Shared Silence

Book 1

Stronger than Truth Trilogy

Lori Bell

Copyright © 2019 by Lori Bell

Cover photograph by CanStock Photo

Printed by CreateSpace

ISBN 978 1096423461

DEDICATION

We do what we do, and take the chances that we take.
To the people in my circle who have taught me how to write
my own life story by the choices I make.

Chapter 1

Fifty. She was a half century old. Her body was telling her things. A once firm belly was softening, and the muscles in her limbs weren't as defined anymore. She still had perky breasts and a curvy rear end. She was more than satisfied with those features. *Not bad.* Still, she was fifty. And it was all going to be downhill from here. *Wasn't it?*

Afton Drury tucked a strand of caramel brown hair behind her ear. Her shoulder-length locks were still damp from the shower as she stood by the coffeemaker on the kitchen counter, taking her first few sips of the hot brew. She drank from the same photo collage mug her now grown children had gifted her, probably fifteen years ago. Those little ones, a boy and a girl, were now twenty-four and twenty-two years old. She was the proud mother of an auto body mechanic and a dental hygienist. It saddened her sometimes to think how quickly the years of watching them grow had flown by. She didn't have regrets though. She had been both a career woman and a doting mother. She thought of her grandmother.

On her deathbed, the eighty-something-year-old spoke of having never done anything for herself. Her entire life's focus had been on being a nurturer to her husband and children. She pushed aside the need for personal fulfillment. Afton would never forget hearing her grandmother say, *"Find something to refuel yourself. You must do that for yourself. Don't live solely for the sake of others. A woman needs more than that, just the same as a man does."* Afton had not forgotten those words or the powerful message from a woman who harbored remorse at the end of her life.

Her outlet, the one thing that refueled Afton for most of her adult life, was photography. She dabbled in it at first, and then freelanced for a local newspaper while in college, before she got serious. Afton Photography was in its twenty-eighth year of business, and still thriving. She grew in creativity and skill, and willingly coasted with the changing times when film quickly was pushed out of the market as digital photography surfaced. To this day, she believed the crisp clear quality of a digital print had not yet matched one captured with film. It was damn close though, and that was enough.

Afton appreciated most things in her life as being enough. She was both grateful and content. And she had accepted what she believed she could not change.

A few more sips of coffee and she would go upstairs to blow dry her hair. She needed to get to the studio to edit her photographs from both a recent high school senior session, and a wedding. Days spent perfecting her work on the computer screen were almost as enjoyable to her as being on a live shoot. She was lost in thought about her plans today when her husband walked into the room.

After spending twenty-five years with the same person, Afton was certain there wasn't anything she didn't know about this man. Thirty minutes before seven o'clock every weekday morning, he emerged from upstairs fully dressed and ready to walk out the door. Today he wore black dress pants and an open collar pale blue dress shirt, with the sleeves already rolled back on his forearms. His dark hair, sporadically salted with gray, was still wet from the shower. And he smelled like talcum powder from his shave. His first steps were typically toward the coffee. Afton always brewed enough for two, but she was the first to drink it.

"Morning birthday girl," he uttered with one casual glance in her direction.

She smirked. "My birthday expired at midnight last night." She thought of the party that her husband and children had thrown for her — with more of their family and close friends.

"It was a good time," he stated, and Afton agreed in her mind, although she stayed silent for a moment. Everyone gathered for dinner at the local Mexican restaurant with a complete margarita bar. Afton stopped herself after having drank three glasses of tequila, but many of her guests had indulged more. And, as usual, her husband was the life of the party. He was never one to get intoxicated, just lively. At one point last evening, a giddy waitress, who had been the recipient of some obvious flirtation from Sam Drury, tugged on Afton's arm and freely commented to her how *she was a lucky woman to be married to such a fun, attentive guy...*

Afton had just enough tequila clouding her good manners to blow past offering an appropriate, agreeable response. Instantly, she heard herself declare, "He's not like that at home."

"It was a wonderful time, thank you and the kids again," Afton eventually responded. She stood a few feet from him, wearing only a pair of cotton panties underneath her white terrycloth robe that frayed just below her knees. It was old, worn, and unbelievably comfortable. Not at all sexy. It had been years since she thought of herself as desirable. Her body didn't respond to her husband anymore, and he certainly never gave her a reason to. Or ever noticed her. Sam Drury was a striking man. Tall. Broad shoulders. Thicker around the middle than he once was, but nothing in excess. They were an attractive pair — they just weren't attracted to each other anymore.

She watched his morning ritual. One piece of dry toast popped up from the toaster. Dark, but not burnt. He took a bite and held it along with his full coffee cup, as he walked toward the door. He would eventually dunk that toasted bread into his coffee before he ate the rest. Probably on his way to the car in the garage.

"Have a good day," she heard herself say to him.

"You too," he responded before he closed the door between the kitchen and the garage. They lived separate lives in the same house. Decade after decade. Much of their time was spent apart now — even inside their home. The psychiatrist and the photographer. He never tried to read her mind, or coerce her to share the depth of her truest feelings. And she gave up a long time ago on capturing that perfect image of him.

Chapter 2

Another birthday celebration, which was a planned dinner solely with her sisters, was something Afton had caught herself thinking about most of the afternoon at her studio. She looked forward to it, yet she dreaded it. Her relationship with both of her younger sisters had fluctuated between being genuinely close and feeling strained through the years. At this stage of their lives, they seemed to pleasantly tolerate each other as if getting together was something they were obligated to do.

In birth order, the three sisters were each five years apart. From youngest to oldest, they were ages forty, forty-five, and fifty. Laney was the middle sister, forty-five years old and blissfully married with twin twelve-year-old sons. She was a junior high school science teacher and her husband was a construction worker. The youngest sister, Skye, had never married, but she was the mother of a two-year-old daughter who was conceived during one of her fleeting relationships. Afton was certain she had planned the pregnancy. Skye wanted to have a baby of her own before her reproductive organs gave up on her, but she couldn't have cared less about having a permanent man in her life. In any case, she had gained a beautiful baby girl and the chance to be a mother.

Afton ordered a glass of white wine with her meal, grilled shrimp kabobs served over a bed of wild grain rice. She took a long swig of the alcohol when her youngest sister mentioned the surprise party last night. The party that neither of her sisters had shown up to celebrate. At the last minute, Skye's baby girl was sick with a high temperature. And Laney's absence was preplanned, as she had hosted some sort of science fair at the junior high school. Both of her sisters were no-shows. They had sent their regrets, via separate messages, and then promptly planned this outing for the following night. It excused the guilt, Afton had assumed, but of course she kept that opinion to herself.

Afton set down her wine glass for a moment. "It wasn't really a surprise. The kids and Sam said they wanted to meet for Mexican food to celebrate my birthday. When I got there, I saw a few familiar cars in the parking lot. I thought it would be too coincidental for our neighbors and Sam's two brothers to all be dining at the same restaurant I was invited to on a milestone birthday."

"You feigned surprised, didn't you?" Laney asked, completely expecting the oldest of the three of them to play along to avoid any disappointed feelings from anyone. It's how Afton was designed. Always putting others first. Avoiding upset. Keeping the peace.

Afton nodded. "It wasn't a big deal to announce that minutes prior I put two and two together in the parking lot."

"Why did you go there alone?" Skye always asked the questions that really didn't need to be spoken. It was almost as if she wanted to hear Afton complain, or break down about the pettiest things. She was a complainer herself, and always enjoyed a good bitch session. But Afton was the complete opposite. She knew how to let things go. She was older...and wiser.

"The kids met me there after work," Afton explained. "Sam too."

"One of my colleagues at school is seeing Sam professionally," Laney offered out of the blue, as if the mere mention of Sam had triggered that information in her mind.

"I hope he can be of some help," Afton stated, which was what she typically said when anyone mentioned Sam's profession as a psychiatrist.

"I cannot imagine him in that element," Skye chimed in, and this wasn't the first time she had brought that up. *Was Sam compassionate enough to be a shrink? Was he truly a good listener?*

"Mental health has always fascinated him," Afton stated, but instantly caught herself thinking about how long it had been since he spoke of the latest findings, or the research he had done in reference to trying to work through people's emotional challenges or psychiatric disorders. She remembered, time and again, seeing the fire in his eyes, that passion he had for helping human beings understand their own mind and body. He had thirty years of experience as a psychiatrist. *Maybe that fire had burned out?* Afton never thought to ask him. But he also never brought up her photography anymore either. Somehow, their careers —and so much else— had become separate from their marriage.

"Can I ask you a personal question, Aft?" Laney was prone to shorten her name, especially when they were younger.

"Ask away," Afton replied, but she took a sip of wine before Laney spoke. The three of them resembled each other· as sisters. They each had hazel eyes and a faint layer of freckles across the bridge of their nose. Just like their mother had. They all had caramel brown hair, but Skye had heavy blonde highlights covering up most of hers. Natural curls were genetic for the Gallant girls too. Consequently, they had invested in flat irons in recent years.

"How intact are you two, in your marriage and all?"

Afton creased her brow. "I'm not sure I fully understand the question. We've been married for twenty-five years. Our kids are grown and will hopefully make us grandparents while we are still young enough to enjoy them. Our careers fulfill us still." Afton could have rambled on, but Skye stopped her. And it wasn't even her initial question. It was Laney's. *Intact? What kind of question was that anyway? A personal one that clearly made Afton uncomfortable.*

"I think what Laney's asking is, are you happy?"

"Girls," Afton spoke to both of them as she had many times before, growing up leading their pack of three. "When you get to be my age, you're content with what you have. It isn't important to seek bigger and better, or wilder and crazier."

"I can't even comprehend that." Skye was ten years younger, and in her mind, she had years left of enjoyment before she settled for anything or anyone. Laney, however, was only five years behind fifty, and she begged to differ.

"Not me. I mean, I understand, but I have an altogether different mindset. I want to be having sex until the very end of my life, wrinkles, imperfections, and all." For a moment, both Afton and Skye only stared at her. Then Skye giggled.

Afton had never said anything about having, or not having sex. *Was she that obvious? The truth was, she wasn't even sure if she had a working vagina anymore. Including the flare-ups and inconveniences of menopause, that sucker was useless to her.*

"I'm sure it will still be happening for you, Laney," Afton began, knowing her middle sister and her husband, Brad, were still hot for each other after fifteen years of marriage. They were just one of those couples. You could see the chemistry between them. Afton was never jealous of it, but she was well aware. "Sex just never did anything for me, if you want me to be honest. I assure you, it's a thing some people can live without." Both of her sisters looked at her with enough sympathy to fill a funeral home.

"And Sam is okay with that?" Skye blurted out. "I mean, does he come on to you and you reject him? Or do you just go through the motions for his sake?"

Afton finished off the wine in her glass. "If you two weren't my sisters, I would get up and leave this table right now. I don't know how we got here, to a subject we haven't talked about since we were hormonal teenagers, but if you both are that curious and must know — I do not have a sex life." It had been years since she and Sam were intimate, but Afton refrained from adding that detail.

The shared silence at their table was brief, but uncomfortable, nonetheless. So, Afton spoke again.

"I know what you're both thinking. Sam must be getting it somewhere else then. I don't believe he's ever been unfaithful to me, but I also do not dwell on it."

"So, you sort of have an open relationship?" Skye asked, sounding entirely too worldly for Afton. And perhaps even for Laney, too, as she had only had sex with one man her entire life. Afton at least had two other lovers in college before she met and married Sam. In her twenties she remembered sex as something she just did. Like the times she occasionally smoked weed, or drank alcohol until she was wasted. Maybe those were the times she welcomed sex?

"Well no," Afton finally answered her. "At least, I don't."

"Right, because you hate sex," Skye clarified.

Afton shrugged her shoulders, and finally this awkward conversation was interrupted by the waiter with their dinner plates.

Afton drove home almost two hours later, thinking. Over thinking. Why did one intrusive question (and a subject matter that eventually passed during their dinner conversation) now weigh so heavily on her mind? She was happy with her life. Content at fifty. But was her marriage intact? Maybe that was something she could ask Sam as a psychiatrist and not as her husband? Her armpits pooled with sweat at the thought as she parked her Highlander in the garage next to her husband's sedan.

Sam was awake and sitting up in their bed, with his laptop overtop the white duvet, resting on his legs. "How was dinner?" He looked above his reading glasses, which sat low on his nose. His dark hair was still damp from the shower and looked as if he had just run his fingers through it instead of using a brush. That look was sometimes boyish, but the deep wrinkles around her husband's eyes and across his forehead caught her eye. He looked older to her just now.

"Really good. I had the shrimp kabobs." After turning her back to him, she placed her shoes on the floor of their walk-in closet. One side was all his, and the other, hers. "We had some deep conversation tonight," she added, keeping herself inside of the closet. A part of her was questioning what in the hell she was doing, blowing this subject wide open with him.

"Oh yeah?" Sam asked, but Afton could tell by the tone of his voice that he had faded from focusing on talking to her, and had already began to regroup his thoughts on work, on the screen in front of him.

Afton bit her lip, and slowly emerged from the closet. She looked at him, and for a moment she was going to just let it go. *He wasn't listening anyway.*

After her long pause, Sam looked at her again. "So, are you going to tell me what the subject matter was between you and your sisters?"

"Well, okay," she said, feeling her heart rate quicken. This was absurd. He was her husband. The father of her children. And, yes, her lover once upon a time. "Sex."

Afton felt her face flush a little. *Ridiculous!* She chided herself. And then she watched Sam shift the laptop on his legs and fold his hands in front of it. "So, tell me, no let me guess. Skye prefers to be on her knees when she doesn't really know the guy all that well... and Laney and Brad continue to mate like rabbits."

Afton's eyes widened. That was true, but those were her sisters he was talking about. "Sam, that's inappropriate," she heard herself say.

"You're right. I apologize. But I'm pretty darn close to accurate, aren't I?" He chuckled under his breath when Afton halfheartedly nodded her head.

"We also talked about my sex life, or they inquired about it," Afton began, feeling entirely too awkward to be having this conversation with him, and wishing she had not brought it up.

Sam only stared at her this time. And his face was expressionless. This was on her mind, so Afton willed herself to continue. But, before she did, Sam spoke for her. "Did you tell your sisters that sex is dreadful for you?" His question sounded borderline snarky, but Afton didn't react to that.

"I would like you to see me as a client right now. If I came to you, and admitted that my husband never touches me... and I really don't do anything to make him want to touch me... would you still say that a marriage like that is intact?"

"Intact, huh?" Sam took off his glasses as he too was questioning that descriptive word. "I think, yes, a marriage can be intact in many other ways. But I also think, as a psychiatrist and as a man, that sex completes a marriage."

So they were not only not intact, but also incomplete? Afton was somewhat taken aback. The fact that they were communicating this way, so openly, had thrown her off as well. It had been a long time. "In your mind then, we are incomplete?" There, she said it.

"We've been married for twenty-five years. I am not looking to change that. You're my wife. This is our life. I've gotten used to the fact that you do not desire me."

"I don't think those are the right words," Afton felt as if she had hurt him. He was a handsome man. Even at fifty-six years old, wearing the effects of Father Time, he was still distinguished and attractive. Afton never sincerely thought of her lack of interest in intimacy that way before. It was never about Sam.

"If you want the truth, Afton, I will share with you how I've felt as your husband. Selfish," he stated bluntly, and she looked confused. "I obviously have reached my climax when we've been intimate. Have you ever had an orgasm? Felt utterly satisfied? Sexually spent? No. I doubt so. Your tension never allowed it. I stopped wanting to feel as if our bodies together, like that, was all about me."

"I'm sorry," Afton heard herself say.

He nodded his head, slowly, but said nothing.

"It's been years, Sam. I imagine your body still has those needs." She paused before she asked him what they both knew was coming next. "Have you been with other women?"

"I think we should close this subject before it becomes hurtful." He already felt like his wife didn't trust him. And Afton suddenly felt betrayed. As well as partially to blame.

Whatever open communication had just taken place between the two of them had instantly gone away again. Afton left his bedside and walked into their master bathroom and closed the door. And before she took off her clothes, she quietly turned the lock.

They were so far from being intact.

Chapter 3

Knox Manning uprooted and moved 7.54 miles from one city to the next. His former life was in Minneapolis. And now he was beginning a new life in Saint Paul. The Twin Cities were less than eight miles apart in Minnesota, but it was enough distance and change for Knox to handle right now. A home in the historic part of Saint Paul was now his new address. It was a splurge of space for only himself, but the decision felt right.

He strolled a cobblestone sidewalk downtown Saint Paul. He looked down at the uneven stones underneath the weathered brown boat shoes on his bare feet. Knox recognized and appreciated the differences in the Twin Cities. The pace was slower where he was now, in Saint Paul, but there were indeed huge draws for people to frequent the museums, the theaters, the sports venues, and more than one urban park. The people just enjoyed those things at a lesser pace there. While Minneapolis was sleek and modern, Saint Paul was rich in culture. Both appealed to Knox. But only one bustling city had been where his wife of eight years wanted to live. Minneapolis was their home until she called it quits and left him when their marriage had succumbed to the strain of infertility. Knox was alone in every life decision again. And to him that felt both isolating and empowering. In his early forties, he really did not want to begin again with his life. But yet here he was.

Knox looked ahead on his path. He watched a woman parallel park a mid-size SUV along the curb. A large, bulky shoulder bag hung from her arm. She held a cup of something and car keys in her hands. An open, outside pocket on her bag was stuffed full of what looked like small white envelopes. When she stepped up onto the curb, a few of those fell out of her bag. She struggled to bend her knees, balancing a full cup of something, as her hands and arms were full, and the larger bag was slipping off her shoulder. She appeared to retrieve what she dropped on the ground as she moved toward the door of a business. Knox looked up at the sign on the building. *Afton Photography.*

Afton managed to unlock the door and enter her studio. By the time Knox was in front of that building and adjacent to the parked car, he looked down, near the front tire, and noticed what looked like a CD sleeve. When she dropped those, she had missed one. He speculated that she was the photographer who owned this business where he stood out front. And he was entirely certain that white sleeve had a CD inside that was important. He bent down near the curb and grabbed it before he walked up to the door of Afton Photography and turned the handle.

The door chimed behind her, as Afton unloaded everything in her arms onto her computer desk for now. She rarely had a prompt customer the second she opened for business at 9 a.m. Most of her business was typically done by appointment. When she turned to greet whoever was walking through her door already, he spoke first when he waved the packaged CD in the air in front of him. She recognized it as her own.

"Found this on the curb out front, and I'm taking a chance that it's likely yours." He grinned.

She laughed before she spoke. It helped to have the obvious Afton Photography stamp in cursive lettering on the outside of the sleeve. "Good guess," she teased, and walked the length of her store to meet him halfway. Her arms were now free, but her body still felt sweaty underneath her clothing from wrestling to carry everything outside in the heat and humidity. Saint Paul was known to be sticky. She noticed this man was feeling it too, as his fitted, white short-sleeve button down shirt clung to him in places she caught herself staring for a moment. His chest was broad and it narrowed down to his abs, but she shook that thought from her head and immediately made eye contact with him. Afton was a business woman, a people person who never met a stranger. She knew many people in this community, but this man was a new face. "Thank you," she said taking the sleeve, and standing in place in the middle of the room with him.

"You're welcome," he looked at his surroundings for a moment. She still needed to turn on all of the lights. "Is this all yours? You're a photographer?"

Afton stepped over to the wall to flip on the light switches. "Yes, my work, my business. I'm Afton Drury." He met her near the wall where she stood. His eyes were momentarily on her work, admiring those wall hangings —both framed photographs and canvases— high above their heads. He turned and reached out his hand to her.

"Knox Manning. A pleasure to meet you, Afton."

For a moment she was self-conscious of her clammy hand, but she joined his regardless. "Are you new to Saint Paul?"

"Yes and no. I've lived in Minneapolis most of my adult life. I've certainly been here, but now I've moved here."

Afton nodded. "Isn't it something how two cities, dubbed twins at that, can be so close in proximity yet vastly different?"

Knox agreed. "Both have perks all their own, too."

His khaki shorts hung long, reaching just above his knees. His boat shoes were trendy. He was tan. So much so that his wavy brown hair looked blond in parts, probably from being touched by the sun. Knox eyed the large photograph of Skye's baby girl on the beach. She wore a little white, ruffled dress, and she was barefoot in the sand with only a blue sky and calm ocean waves in the background. She watched him take in the photograph.

"She's a beautiful baby," he eventually commented. Knox never asked if the baby was hers. There wasn't an appropriate way to phrase that. *Grandbaby?* She looked past the prime of motherhood, but she was a striking woman around his age, if Knox had to guess. *Maybe a smidge older.*

"My niece, Bella," Afton beamed.

"She looks like a lot of fun. I'm sure being in the sand was an adventure for that photo shoot."

"For me and her!" Afton laughed out loud, and Knox noticed the catching way that she threw her head back, and how the laughter met her eyes. *Genuine emotion.* He chuckled in turn because he couldn't help himself.

"I'll bet. I mean, I don't personally know," he suddenly looked serious, "but I imagine babies to be such a joy." He stopped at that. Halted his thoughts and his spoken words. Being a father once gradually and intensely became his greatest dream, but it just never happened. Little people were drawn to him, and he to them. But Knox finally believed that he wasn't meant to have his own.

"No children of your own?" It was a natural question that perhaps he had even set himself up for, so Knox just responded the only way he knew how. Honestly.

"No. My ex-wife and I had fertility issues." It felt stranger for him to say, ex-wife, than to reveal they struggled with infertility. But that was in the past. Both his marriage and his chance to become a father.

Afton tried not to allow her facial expression to react. She was taken aback, and embarrassed. "Oh my gosh. I'm very sorry. How insensitive of me." *Such a stupid question. We never know what others are going through.*

"Not at all. You're making conversation. I brought up the baby in the photograph on your wall. It's a part of life, Afton. We all have struggles. If we cannot be authentic, we may as well not even bother. I'm not one of those people who's going to pretend that life is perfect."

She admired his direct honesty, because it wasn't something she did. She didn't open up to complete strangers, or really all that much to anyone. It was unfamiliar to her to express her personal feelings. "Life certainly isn't faultless for anyone," she stated, because it was true and she didn't know what else to say. Knox immediately sensed her uneasiness.

He couldn't help wondering what imperfections had crept into her life and clung to her thoughts and feelings. To her heart and soul. He wasn't ready to ask her though. He was forthcoming, not intrusive. "I should let you be productive," he started to back away from the wall they stood near.

"It's fine. Thank you for returning the disk I dropped outside. I would have been searching for it eventually."

"You're welcome, Afton."

See you around, he thought, but didn't say it.

Welcome to the other Twin City, she refrained from verbalizing, because inside her head the echo of it sounded cheesy.

The door chimed again and he was gone.

Afton tugged at the scoop neckline of her black lyrca top that she had paired with cropped white denim and low-heeled black sandals. She would need to check the thermostat in there. Her body temperature had not cooled down since she stepped inside the store. And had an unexpected visitor.

Knox continued walking the cobblestone sidewalk outside of Afton Photography. *He would need an excuse to see her again.* That, he knew for sure.

Chapter 4

A few hours later, Knox was still taking in the city. He had frequented Saint Paul a multitude of times throughout his life, having lived so close. But this was different. This city was his home now. He appreciated it more. He wanted to soak up what he could before he returned to work after a month-long leave of absence. During that time, Knox had found and bought a house. He began his search in the historic part of Saint Paul. He always wanted a home with some substance, with a tasteful stamp of days gone by on the exterior. And Knox wanted that very same feeling when he stepped foot inside. He found a folk Victorian house on Holly Avenue that had spoken to him. The very same day he met the realtor, he purchased it. The house was built in 1883 and still had casement windows, a tiled fireplace in the upstairs master bedroom, and he was fascinated with an original second staircase hidden behind the hallway closet, which he was told was no longer used, but it descended to the kitchen. There was an original sleeping porch that had been restored too. Knox imagined the stories those walls could tell. He hoped to make a few memories of his own there.

In the past few weeks, he had settled in fairly quickly. He unpacked for one. He brought a few pieces of furniture with him after the divorce, and he furnished the rest of his home with everything new. A part of him wondered if his ex-wife would approve of his new, but older, living quarters. Probably not, he thought to himself, as she was more of a modern-day woman. He scuffed the bottoms of his boat shoes as he walked an open path at Mears Park, located in the heart of downtown Saint Paul's Lowertown district. There were more parks in that city than he could have possibly imagined, but this one piqued his interest online when he read that it had a stream running diagonally through the park. That, he wanted to see.

Something he was not expecting to see in the middle of the park was what looked like preparation for a makeshift wedding ceremony, back-dropped by the park's seasonal flower garden he recalled reading about online. His path zigzagged a little before bringing him closer. There were no guests or ceremony in progress just yet. He saw the white folding chairs aligned, the flowers, the place at the helm of the scene where two people would commit their lives to each other and make promises they intended to keep. Knox knew how that didn't always work out. Two people were talking in the distance. He assumed one of them had arranged those fresh flowers as bookends for each row of white chairs. He planned to keep moving on the path along the stream, but that's when he noticed another person readying for the wedding scene was a photographer. Luck was on his side, as he didn't have to hope to see her again. He had already.

Knox stepped aside, off the path for a moment as he balanced on one of the large rocks bordering the stream. Two women in tank tops and spandex shorts were speed walking by, while Knox stood stationary. One of them awed when she noticed there was going to be a wedding ceremony, right there in the park.

When Knox resumed walking, he glanced in Afton's direction again and she was gone. He looked harder and noticed she was crotched down between a row of chairs. When she stood, her camera dangled from a thick strap around her neck. He also saw a few early guests arriving from the east side of the flower garden. Afton was working, and Knox felt awkward about interrupting. *He should just walk by.* Less than thirty seconds later, he heard his name.

The wedding planner had noticed him.

"Dr. Manning?"

Knox stopped in his tracks, literally, as a middle-aged woman waved at him from a distance. And now, Afton had also turned to look in his direction.

He stepped closer to the wedding area. "Dr. Manning. I'm Rita Wright. A patient of yours at Regency Minneapolis." Of course she was. Knox had recognized her now.

"It's nice to bump into you. I see you're working a wedding out here." He assumed again that she was the wedding coordinator, or the actual florist. She was holding a bundle of fresh flowers in her hand now.

"Yes. Good to see you. I hope you haven't left Regency. Rumor has it that you took an indefinite leave of absence." Knox could tell that Afton was listening. She was within earshot, as she pretended to toy with her camera lens. Perhaps she really was prepping her equipment for the wedding shoot.

"I will be back, Rita. Soon, actually." That was all Knox offered, and with good reason. His divorce and recent move weren't banner news in the Twin Cities, and certainly not something he wanted to discuss in his professional world.

"Well that's wonderful to hear! And, you just take your time getting back on your feet again. There's a good woman out there for you, Dr. Manning." And there it was. News of his divorce. The headline. Spoken about to his face by a patient, nonetheless.

Afton kept her eyes down, purposely fidgeting with her camera. *So he was a doctor?* She recalled him mentioning an ex-wife, but never assumed he was newly divorced. The wedding planner, and patient of his, obviously had very little couth. Afton was embarrassed for her. The man had a right to take a personal leave from his job without revealing the details.

Afton looked up when they parted, and Knox had glanced her way. She watched him raise his hand in the air to wave at her. She called out a friendly greeting to him. "Hello again..."

Knox stepped further into the wedding area, where only a few guests had started to make their way to their seats.

"Yes, we meet again," he said to her. "On a whim, I chose to take a walk in one of the dozens of parks in this city and it looks like I picked a bustling one today. You're shooting a midday wedding here?"

Afton smiled. "It's going to be *beautiful*," she emphasized, "but this is one of those times I'm happiest to be behind the lens. The humidity is thick out here, and I already feel like a sweaty mess." Knox watched her dab the perspiration above her brow with the back of her bare hand. The walking path he had been on was covered by shade trees and much more pleasant than where they were standing in direct sunlight. He hoped for some cloud cover for the nuptials, since a sudden drop in the humidity level was unlikely.

Knox chuckled. "I hear you. Let's hope the bride and groom aren't too overdressed." He imagined the tailcoat tuxedo he had been told to wear on his wedding day. He, however, had gotten married in a Catholic church with the comfort of air conditioning.

"I was with them earlier, and I think they are well prepared. Lovely young couple with lots of hopes and dreams." Knox caught himself glancing at Afton's hand. *No ring.*

"We all start out that way, don't we," he stated, and he was secretly wishing to know her story. *Had she ever been married? Was she in a long-term relationship where she had someone to be her forever date?* Knox's divorce was barely final. He, however, pushed that reminder from his thoughts because there was no specific time frame for moving on. And besides, he enjoyed talking to Afton Drury. And yes, he was already attracted to her. The way her blouse clung to her full chest made him think about what it would be like to peel away that layer. Sex had become obligated and always preplanned between him and his ex-wife in recent years. *They were trying to make a baby.* That was the only focus he had when he made love. The pleasure in it had long been gone.

"I suppose so," Afton halfheartedly agreed. "People grow and change so much, and it is a blessing when a couple can master that in sync with each passing year." Knox pondered if she was speaking from experience in a remorseful way.

Clusters of more people began to file in around them. Knox watched Afton turn her head and do a sweep of her surroundings. "Looks like you have work waiting," he told her, because he wanted to be polite and not intrude on her time. But he would have rather kept talking to her.

"Stay and watch, if you'd like. People do it all the time. It's a public place."

"Seriously?" Knox certainly wanted to stay.

"Absolutely. I'll show you a few frames on my camera after it's over." She was a proud and confident professional, and Knox immediately liked that about her.

He had an open invitation, from her, to stay. And to see her again after the wedding ceremony.

Afton honestly never thought twice about it. But Knox certainly did.

Chapter 5

The outdoor wedding was breathtaking and flawless and everything a wedding should be. But Knox wasn't paying much attention to any of that detail. He watched the photographer the entire time. Afton captured the expected moments. The bride walking down the aisle on the arm of presumably her father. The groom's face when he saw his bride. The tears in their eyes as they recited their vows, and slipped rings on each other's hands. Knox watched Afton use a tripod for specific shots, and switch between a telephoto and a wide-angle lens. She kept her distance and was respectful not to get in the way of the ceremony, or the crowd's view. But she also made no apologies for the job she was there to do. Timing was everything, even during a routine wedding ceremony. And Afton seemed to be in the right position for all of the key moments. She was a seasoned photographer, no doubt.

Once the ceremony concluded, applause and cheers erupted, and the final music note was cut. Knox noticed Afton had followed the newly married couple off the site. And he was waiting for her when she returned less than ten minutes later. The two of them, and the clean-up crew, were the only ones left.

"You waited," she said, feeling a little surprised, but she hadn't forgotten her invitation to him. *Maybe he did want to see her photographs.*

"Of course." Although he wondered where everyone had gone off to and if Afton still had a full day of work ahead of her with the wedding party.

"That's a wrap for me. I took all of their photos prior to the ceremony. I just wanted one final shot now as they boarded their limo for lunch, before they are off to the airport."

"No such thing as a reception anymore?"

"Not with this group, I guess. There really is no blueprint anymore. Couples just do what they want. And I personally think that is liberating."

"Agreed," Knox told her, as she started to gather her camera equipment.

"Hey wait, when do I get a sneak peek?" Knox was serious about seeing her work, even if she had feigned that she forgot mentioning it.

"Oh," she laughed. "Sure." He watched her scan the display screen on the back of her digital Canon 50D. "This, I think, is my money shot." She shared the view of the image with him.

It was a photo of the bride and groom, just as they turned to face their family and friends after being pronounced as husband and wife. They joined hands and lifted their linked arms together, high in the air. As if to say, *Look at us! We did it. We are in this forever.* And there was evident love and laughter in their eyes.

"There's a lot of feeling in that photo," Knox described what he saw. "The emotion on their faces and in their actions, joined hands and all, speaks love and hope for the future."

"You see what I see," Afton stated, feeling pleased with herself for capturing that special moment.

"I do," he told her, and stared at her for a moment longer than he should have. Afton ceased eye contact with him then.

"I should pack up my things," she suggested.

"You're a natural at what you do, Afton Drury. I'm impressed. Thanks for inviting me to watch." He didn't mean the wedding ceremony.

"I learned many years ago that timidity will not get the shot. Although I don't consider myself a bold person, I know how to be, to capture the work I want."

Knox liked how she revealed something personal about herself. It seemed easy for her to talk about her work, more so than herself. He wanted to know more. He wished to know Afton Drury's story. Strangely, Knox felt as if time was of the essence with this woman. In the very same day, he had both met her and coincidentally crossed paths with her again.

"I remember those days, early in my medical career, when I willed myself to act confident. I wasn't, but I wanted to be perceived as I was. The career I was beginning depended on it. I eventually got past that. It's really good for the self-esteem when you are successful at helping people heal." He grinned.

Afton thought of her husband, a doctor of mental health. "What kind of doctor are you?"

"Orthopedic."

Afton nodded. She was impressed. "A surgeon too?"

"Yes," Knox smiled. They were still standing near the rows of chairs that needed to be folded and stacked and stored away somewhere. They weren't in anyone's way, but there were a few people around them, cleaning up the area. "I've missed it actually. My leave is about up, as you may have heard Rita and I discussing."

"She was a tad intrusive, if you ask me," Afton offered, suddenly feeling as if Knox was an old friend she could say anything to.

Knox chuckled. "Sometimes people just want to know things. Those questions on their minds need to be answered. Would you think I was being intrusive if I asked you more about your life?"

Afton looked down at her camera bag on one of the chairs. A moment later, she turned back to him. "Not much to tell, really."

"Have you ever been married?"

Afton realized she had not worn her wedding ring. That gold band and single pear-shaped two-carat diamond soldered together twenty-five years ago. It was habit for her to remove her wedding set and forget to put it back on. She was certain she would find it later, placed on one of the cornered window sills above the kitchen sink.

"Yes, and I have two grown children," Afton answered. "My son is twenty-four, and my daughter is twenty-two. I just turned fifty, in case you're wondering."

Knox chuckled at her honesty. "Well you look radiant and entirely too young to be the mother of adult children." It was a compliment that she was willing to accept. *At fifty, who didn't want to soak up those flattering words?*

"Since we are revealing our numbers, I'm merely months from forty-four." She smiled. He should meet her little sister, who was closer to his age. Skye had a baby —something he desperately wanted— and she likely would be willing to bear more. Too bad he wasn't at all her type. *But who's type was Knox Manning?* She felt a flutter in her belly. And she tried to ignore the attraction. This was unfamiliar, uncharted territory for her. *It was harmless flirting, really.* But she liked it, nonetheless.

"Such youth," she teased him, and he laughed.

"Hardly, but I don't focus on the number."

Afton nodded, as she zipped the last of her equipment, packed securely into her camera bag. The tripod was collapsed and currently taking up space on two chairs.

"Can I help you carry that to your car?" he offered.

"No, I'm quite self-sufficient, but thank you." She doubted he was parked on the east side of the premises anyway, and it was unnecessary to make him go out of his way.

"I understand," he told her, as he watched her shoulder the camera bag and carry the collapsed tripod rods across her forearms.

She looked up at him as they were about to part ways. She guessed him to be six feet tall next to her five-five frame. She caught herself thinking about details like that with him. His sun-kissed skin. His dark blue eyes. Afton realized she was studying him like a subject she focused on through her camera lens. She enjoyed his company. He was truly a breath of fresh air. And now it seemed strange to say, *see you around, or it was nice meeting you...*

So instead, she spoke something packed with a little more sincerity. "I hope you find what you're looking for here in Saint Paul."

At first he only smiled. Her words were genuine, and beyond meaningful to him. "I appreciate that more than you know," he replied, and then added, "After today, I think I'm off to a promising start."

She giggled a little, and really didn't read too much into his words, as she turned and walked away from him.

A smile stayed with him for a long time. *Afton Drury. He liked her name. It was chic, like her.* She was a naturally beautiful woman. Those pale freckles that formed across the bridge of her nose were adorable. She had laugh lines and crow's feet on her otherwise ageless face. Her body had not gone unnoticed to him either. The way her curvy backside looked in that pair of white denim crops was an image that would hold him over until the next time he saw her again. He sensed that Afton was a woman who didn't embrace too much too soon. But he could have been mistaken. He primarily had felt the same way about beginning his life over. Until he met her today.

Chapter 6

When Afton reached her car, she started the engine and turned the air conditioner on full blast as she retrieved her cell phone that she had left in the glove compartment. She didn't welcome interruptions while she was working. And now, she had a rare text message in the middle of the day from Sam, which she noticed he sent two hours ago.

Last minute dinner plans. We are going out with the Robertsons. Casual dress, Jess said to tell you.

Mark and Jess Robertson were long-time friends of theirs. They had raised their children throughout the same years, and Mark and Sam golfed together. Afton enjoyed the Robertsons. She and Jess were not super close girlfriends, but they easily conversed and effortlessly picked up right where they left off whenever they saw each other no matter how much time had passed.

Afton replied to Sam's text.

Just shot a wedding. I'll leave the studio at 4 to be ready in time for dinner.

Saint Paul Grill on Market Street was on their list, a compilation of restaurants that the four of them frequented often. Afton already knew what she was going to order. The rotisserie chicken, which was served as a half chicken in a light pan sauce alongside sautéed baby broccoli florets with long, thin stalks. She had skipped lunch today, as she was working the wedding, so her stomach was rumbling just thinking about eating. A few minutes after five o'clock, she received a text from Sam.

Meet you there.

It was typical of him to run late, and Afton was accustomed to escorting herself pretty much everywhere. Sam's office was furnished with a personal shower and he always had an extra shirt or pair of jeans with him. He was self-sufficient, and Afton had appreciated that about her husband. He wasn't helpless or needy. She counted that as one of the things that worked in their marriage. Many couples were off balance, as one or the other had a much greater need. Afton definitely could name a few people she knew who acted as the doting, caretaker wife. Sam didn't need her to take care of him.

Afton actually had shown up last to the restaurant, because she had poured herself a glass of Moscato while getting ready and wanted to finish drinking it as she sat at the granite-top, L-shaped island in her kitchen. She was lost in thought for awhile. The wedding this afternoon had been exactly as she had imagined it would be. After viewing the photographs prior to editing, she felt as if she outdid herself on some of the images. *To success!* She had toasted herself. She also thought of Knox Manning. *What a breath of fresh air,* he was.

She joined the party of three already in progress with drinks on the table. Sam stood up when he saw her. He still had some of the old-school gentleman qualities in him. "Hi honey," he greeted her the enthusiastic way he always did when they were in public. Terms of endearment. Holding her eyes with his. Squeezing her hand. "It's not like you to be the last to arrive. Traffic?" Afton looked at their friends. Jess, with her dark, long hair in big loose curls that reached halfway down her back. Her smile was wide. All flawless, white teeth. Afton always thought of her as a cross between Julia Roberts and Cindy Crawford. She wasn't a small-framed woman by any means, but she was well proportioned with long limbs, and a lean torso. Afton had bigger boobs though, and she always chuckled to herself at that thought. It wasn't a competition. They were friends. But Afton still boosted her own confidence with that truth. Mark was a big man. He had the neck of a football player. And for some reason, Afton never failed to always notice his hands. They were dimpled at the knuckles. He was tall at six-four and his belly hung way over his belt. Sam, just two inches shorter, and carrying only a rounded pooch at his waist, looked small compared to him.

"No, I can't blame traffic. It was the glass of Moscato in the kitchen that I had to finish." They all laughed in unison as both Afton and Sam sat down.

"Let's get you another one of those!" Jess called out, and Afton didn't object as she settled on the chair in between her husband and her girlfriend. She respected Jess, and enjoyed their conversations, especially about their careers. Jess was a speech pathologist at the same middle school where Afton's sister, Laney taught.

"How was the wedding shoot in the park today?" Afton turned to Sam when he spoke to her. If they had been at home, he never would have inquired. She was surprised he was listening a few days ago when she told him the midday wedding was taking place in Mears Park.

"It was wonderful. Hot and humid, but so perfect in every other way. I'm going to blare my own horn and say that I outdid myself on some of the photos."

Jess clapped her hands together, and instantly mentioned wanting to see a few of those images sometime. Afton grinned. "Your job certainly is pure fun, I would think," Mark stated, and Afton nodded in agreement.

"What? Yours isn't?" Sam chuckled when he directed that question at Mark, who was a mortician and third generation funeral director of Robertson Funeral Home in Saint Paul.

"It's not always lively," Mark deadpanned, and the rest of them either groaned or rolled their eyes.

"Let's see if we can get our waitress over here to order some dinner for these beautiful women," Sam boasted as Mark waved his arm in the air for the young woman bringing drinks to an adjacent table from theirs. And Afton briefly caught a look on Jess' face. Sam called her a beautiful woman, and she had given him a wink. A wink wasn't alarming. Afton was hardly insecure. And most times she ignored her husband's flirtatious personality when they were in public. It was just a show anyway. He was entirely more reserved in private. But it was Sam's reaction to Jess' sexy little wink that Afton turned her head in time to see. A look that Afton saw him give their friend was familiar. He once looked at her the same way. With longing in his eyes.

Dinner continued with good conversation and more of Sam's boisterous stories and a few inappropriate jokes. They ordered a final round of drinks after their meal, which was in sync with Mark's cell phone ringing. Back in the day, he would say, his father and grandfather had pagers for emergency calls.

"I have a customer," Mark stood up at the table, excusing himself. He referred to a deceased body that needed to be transported to the funeral home. They were used to this happening on their date nights, quite often actually, and Jess spoke first. "As usual, I have a ride."

They all said a quick goodbye to him, and Sam turned to the women he was left alone with at the table. "Ready when you are," he said to Jess, "and I know my wife will want to get home to get a jumpstart on her beauty sleep." It was something he said before, and it had never been an issue with Afton. She almost always drove herself and was anxious to go home to get ready for bed. But this time, Afton dwelled. Her husband often acted as if he was rescuing his buddy's wife when he drove her home like a good pal and a gentleman would.

"I am tired," Afton heard herself say.

"I need to visit the ladies' room really quick," Jess stood up, as Afton did too, and they shared a close hug goodbye. When Jess ran off, Afton put her handbag on her shoulder. Sam remained seated. He was drinking the last of the whiskey and water in his glass. No one but his wife was left to put on a show for.

"See you at home," Afton told him.

He nodded. "Drive safe. I could be an hour or so. I left my suit at the office and I need to drop it off at the dry cleaners in the morning." Afton nodded. That, too, was nothing new. But this time the words, that used to be just words, were circling around in her mind and lingering there. Lingering just like the inappropriate look of longing that Afton witnessed Sam give their friend, Jess.

Afton got to her car and immediately got inside and drove out of the parking lot. She then parked directly across the street at a seafood restaurant. She turned off the engine and killed the headlights. Not even five minutes passed, and she watched the two of them come out of the restaurant together.

Sam had his arm on the small of her back the entire time they walked, alongside of each other. He opened her car door for her. Jess pressed her hand to his chest. She was tall, even more so wearing heels with her dark-washed denim. She nearly stood eye to eye with Sam. She watched them look down in unison and laugh about something. And then she saw Sam shift himself through his jeans. In public, he touched his manhood. In front of their friend, Jess Robertson. He was aroused. They appeared to be giddy about it. Afton had just witnessed an intimate moment between her husband and her friend. And something told her, as disgusting as it was, the two of them had likely done much more behind closed doors.

Afton waited for them to leave in her husband's car. And then she followed.

Sam did drive her home, as he said he would. But he didn't drop Jess off at the door. He parked his car on the driveway and walked inside the house with her. And little did they both know that the small lamp the Robertson's kept lit all the time in their front window had illuminated the windows just enough to see inside, through the slanted open blinds. There was a narrow window to the left of the front door. Through it, Afton could see her husband reaching for the hem of her sleeveless sweater and lifting it up and off her body. He kissed her lips first, long and hard, as she pressed the barely B cups of her padded bra against his chest.

And then Afton drove the hell away from there.

Chapter 7

An hour later, she was upstairs in their bed, awake, when Sam came home. She sat upright, watching the TV that was mounted high on their bedroom wall.

"You're still awake?" he spoke first. Afton looked at him. Really looked at her husband. He was dressed the same as he was at the restaurant. And not a hair on his head was out of place. *Should she have known? Had there been other obvious signs like the one Afton intercepted tonight?* She never obsessed over their lack of intimacy. She did know there was the possibility that Sam was unfaithful to her. And she felt ridiculous thinking this way, but the idea of a quickie with his secretary or a complete stranger was easier to take than knowing Jess Robertson was screwing her husband. Her friend, of all people. They weren't can't-live-without-you best friends, but they were somewhat close. Afton enjoyed her. *She was fun and kind and caring and just lovely. Her only flaw was her small chest for chrissakes! The woman helped little elementary kids find their voice for a living!* She wasn't awful. And yet, Afton found herself feeling more bothered by Jess' actions than her own husband's. Of course Sam was to blame. *He had probably seduced her... how many times ago?* Even still. Afton wasn't jealous. She was hurt. Because she had lost a friend tonight.

41

"Did Jess get home okay?" she asked him, feigning concern for the woman her husband had just gotten naked with.

"Yes, a little tipsy but I got her to her front door safely." He chuckled, and Afton winced at the image of the two of them just inside that front door. *Her shirtless friend, and her husband with the strained bulge in his pants.*

"She's a beautiful woman," Afton told him, as he began to make his way across their bedroom floor, toward the master bathroom.

"What?" he slowed his pace but didn't stop.

"Jess. I think she's beautiful, don't you?"

Afton watched her husband shrug his shoulders. "Sure, I guess so, yeah. Mark is a lucky guy." It was easier to bring his buddy into this. Afton understood his mindset. Sam was a psychiatrist after all. He knew the mind exceptionally well and how to play those games with it.

"I mean, really, there isn't a flaw on that woman. I'm not envious. I'm praising her. I really do love her. I never truly thought about it before tonight, but she's one of my closest girlfriends."

Sam nodded. "We've shared a lot of good times with Jess and Mark."

"We sure have," Afton agreed, and paused, and that's when Sam used her brief silence as his chance to escape. He wasn't able to exhale the breath he had been holding until he closed the door and turned on the shower water. *It was nothing,* he told himself. *Afton had no idea about them.*

He and Jess Robertson had been involved for more than a decade. They were sexually compatible. They weren't in love, they were not a couple, nor did they want to be. They had no intentions to ever leave their spouses or change their lives as they were. It was a secret pact, a risky agreement they made years ago. Neither of them had ever been unfaithful with anyone else. And, oddly, for them, carrying on with only each other felt justified.

The following morning, Afton left the house without making coffee. She simply got out of bed and brushed her teeth and washed her face before she donned capri black leggings with a sports bra and tank top. She tightly laced her tennis shoes downstairs and then got into her car to drive to Mears Park. The walking trail there yesterday looked like something she should be enjoying. Exercise was not her calling, but this was one of those times when she needed to clear her mind. A new, bright sky was dawning as her feet hit the paved trail. There were more people out there than she had expected. Some ran alone, some walked in pairs. Afton didn't want to be alone right now, but she was. She wished she could call one of her sisters and confide to them about last night. But, Laney worked at the same school as Jess. She didn't want to tempt her to tell just one other person and have that rumor begin. And Skye would only say she called it. She suspected Sam as a man getting it somewhere else. So Afton just kept walking, and rehashing her thoughts.

An hour passed. It was quiet out there. It was as if most of the people on the trail had gone home to get ready for work. Afton wasn't in a hurry to go home to shower or go to work. She would open her studio later this morning. Right now, she wanted to be unreachable, as her cell phone was in her car's glove compartment again.

There was a bench under a shade tree ahead of her. She had passed it several times this morning. This time, she sat down on it to rest. She must have been lost in thought when she heard her name. Just a short distance away, he was wearing gray running shorts and a red dry-fit t-shirt that was wet across the chest from perspiration.

"Afton?"

"Knox." She smiled.

"We have to stop meeting like this," he stated, teasing. He hardly meant a word of that. But honestly he had not expected to see her out there this morning. He had actually toyed with the idea of calling her business number just to say hello, and maybe ask her out to lunch as an excuse to talk to her again.

"I'll admit I don't typically do this. I've always claimed to be allergic to fitness."

He waved a hand in front of his face. "You look great as you are."

She felt her cheeks flush, and tried to ignore the heat from how it felt to be complimented by him.

"I did make good use of the walking trail. I just now sat down for a break," she wanted to clarify.

"Care if I join you?" Knox asked. She scooted over to make room for him as she was seated in the middle. Knox sat and lifted the hem of his shirt to wipe the sweat from his forehead. She caught a glimpse of his chest then, and felt something stir, low in her body. This didn't happen to her. She was clearly annoyed with the unfamiliar pangs of lust. So much so that she wiggled in place on the bench, as sort of a way to stop those feelings. Knox had not noticed as he dried his face. "I apologize if I reek," he stated to get the awkward out of the way.

He didn't.

Afton giggled. "Me too!"

She didn't either.

They shared silence for a moment. He liked the way her hair curled when it was damp with sweat. She hadn't pulled it up or tied it back, so there were strands of random curls matted to her neck and forehead. And that line of freckles on her nose was more visible sans makeup.

"Something's on your mind," Knox made what he thought was an obvious observation. And Afton was touched. No one really could read her. Not well anyway. Or perhaps she didn't want to be analyzed and figured out. It made her uncomfortable. But, with Knox, that feeling was different. And she said so.

"Actually, yes."

"Do you want to tell me about it?"

"I don't really talk about my private feelings too often. I don't know how good I'll be at it," she confessed.

"Try me."

He had great legs. She looked down and noticed his tanned skin and formed quad and calf muscles. Features always caught her eye. It was the photographer in her. This man was a work of art. She suppressed a grin which stemmed from her last thought.

Afton started to tell him what was weighing on her mind. *Because what did she have to lose?* She raised her left hand to tuck a strand of hair behind her ear. Knox's eyes widened. She was perplexed at his sudden reaction for a second, until she realized that last night at dinner she had worn her wedding ring and kept it on while she slept.

"You're married?" Knox asked outright, because thoughts always turned into words for him. Communication was a strong suit. And he suddenly felt let down that he had not known this. *Afton was married? How had he missed that significant fact? Or why had she kept it from him?* He feared, no, he knew, that this was going to change things. *How could it not? Hadn't she felt the same budding feelings as he did*? He forced himself to give her the chance to speak.

Afton fingered her wedding ring. "I don't always wear it," she began. "I *am* married. For twenty-five years now. Sam is a doctor too, a psychiatrist here in Saint Paul. I don't know how to say this without embarrassing myself but, with you, telling you something so personal, it just feels easy. We are not intimate, and have not been for a very long time."

"So you have some sort of open relationship?" he asked, and Afton thought of Skye. Younger people's minds were just wired differently. And Knox was several years younger than her.

46

"I don't, no," she abruptly answered him, "and to be honest, I never really wondered about Sam being unfaithful to me. Or, I didn't care." She knew that last part was untrue. Last night, however, her mindset changed. She was bothered by it, especially by Jess' betrayal. She never ceased eye contact with Knox as she continued to explain something so terribly personal. "I don't feel desired. Sex just isn't on my radar. I'm fifty years old for crying out loud."

"Don't," he stopped her. He didn't want to hear her talk like that. Especially since he was attracted to her from the moment they met. "Age is just a number, remember? You are a beautiful, attractive woman. I don't know how to convince you of that, other than to say that I have intense feelings for you." He wanted to reach for her hand, and so he did. She was a little jumpy, and tense at first, before she felt herself relax to his touch.

It was as if a fire, no, a full-blown inferno, blazed inside of her. She felt like a hormonal teenager all over again, not knowing what to do with the feelings that both allured and frightened her. She allowed him to touch her hand.

"We went out to dinner last night with friends of ours, another couple that has been in our lives for well over a decade." Knox wondered where she was going with this, but the intensity in her eyes forced his silence as he only listened. "I caught a look between my husband and my friend, Jess. It was enough to make me follow them after we left the restaurant. Not to confuse you, but our friend Mark is a funeral director who got called away for an emergency. My husband and I drove separate to dinner, as he came straight from work."

"So your husband," Knox felt repulsed to say those words. He didn't want this woman to be committed to another man. *Taken.* But, perhaps, she was trying to tell him that she wasn't. "Did he drive your friend home?"

Afton nodded. "It's not something new. He's offered before. Stupid me, I guess. This time, I followed them. I watched them step into her house. Her husband was obviously going to be gone for awhile, and they knew the amount of time they had to be together. They were all over each other after barely getting through the front door." Afton moved her hand from his and brushed a defiant curl from hanging over her eye.

"I'm sorry," Knox offered.

"Don't be. The odd thing about it is I feel more betrayed by my friend than I do by my own husband. I don't want him, like that, anymore. I suppose I'm partly to blame for forcing him to stray."

Knox shook his head. "That's absurd."

"Is it?" she asked. "I have not been a good wife. I've never enjoyed sex."

Knox took a moment to process her words, and he surprised himself how much he understood. "My ex-wife used to schedule our love making. We wanted to conceive a child. We got to the point of just simply going through the motions. I had to think of anything or anyone, something I'm ashamed to admit, just to power through and finish, if you will."

"You're a man... you're supposed to enjoy it. It's sex."

"But I didn't. So, I guess what I want you to understand is... you are not abnormal. And so what if you are fifty years old? You still can feel desire and be wanted by someone else." And he didn't mean her husband.

Afton looked down at the ground underneath her tennis shoes while Knox continued to speak to her. "I want to ask you something, and for the first time in my life I don't know how to put the words together without sounding completely crazy, or downright sneaky." She looked over at him, seated beside her. They were not touching, but their bodies were close. "Would you give me the chance to get to know you better? Not publicly. I would never risk ruining your reputation here. We could have dinner at my place, or just talk somewhere private like we are right here?"

"A part of me wants to say... I'm married," she admitted. "Is this wrong, Knox? Is it absolutely insane that I want to get to know you better, too? I am beginning to feel things for you that I could so easily get caught up in. If exploring that is wrong... well then I never again want to be right in my whole entire life." Maybe she had finally reached a point in her fifty years where she understood when something felt right, then nothing else mattered. It was a dangerous way to think and feel. But damn it, she was there and embracing it.

He smiled at her. "I really don't care about right or wrong, or anyone's conscience right now. Afton... I want to kiss you. I want to show you how right two people can make each other feel."

She felt sweat pool underneath her arms and in between her breasts. Her heartbeat quickened. The v between her legs tightened deep inside. This was insanity for her. And she was dangerously drawn to it. To him. She never stopped him when he moved closer.

There was no one else around when his lips brushed over hers. It was light and tender and as if an electric current had radiated through her veins. She kissed him back with slightly parted lips over his. He teased that opening with his tongue. She met him there and opened her mouth further. He took this slow. So slow she felt her desire screaming inside for more. Their tongues touched. He deepened the kiss first and then she followed. She was breathing heavily and he was reacting by giving her more. They were making out on the park bench like horny teenagers in lust. Their hands never reached for or touched each other the entire time. And by the time they parted, their lips were red and puffy.

"I don't want to stop," he admitted, "but we should." She knew he meant that someone could come upon them, and see what they were doing.

She sighed for a moment, feeling completely overwhelmed with her newfound feelings. This was foreign to her. She had never been kissed like that before. Or had that strong of a reaction to it. "I need to tell you how I feel right now. I'm overwhelmed. In a good way, I suppose, because I want to get in the backseat of my car with you more than you know."

He chuckled. He couldn't help himself. She grinned in embarrassment. "There is no way that I will take you, for our first time, like that." She thought of them being together more than once, and him foreseeing it precisely that way. "You deserve to be cherished and treasured, and for a man to take his time on every inch of you. I want that privilege."

She wanted to go there with him. *All the way there.* He was younger. Incredibly sexy. And Afton was thrilled with herself for being capable of feeling like this. *Finally!* She truly wasn't dead inside. A small part of her thought of this way of thinking as getting back at Sam, whether she would admit that or not. But the rest of her wanted this for herself. *What would be the harm in having one of those open relationships like the younger generation was caught up in?*

Chapter 8

They left the park after having exchanged phone numbers. Afton felt nervous as she drove home. It was after eight o'clock in the morning and she knew Sam would have already left for work. It wasn't until she pulled into the garage when she retrieved her cell phone from inside of the glove compartment that she saw a missed call from him. He left a voicemail. She sat in her car and listened to Sam's message.

"Afton, where are you? It's unlike you not to be home when I leave for work. And you never go without coffee in the morning." A detail about her that he was well aware of, but they were so far from recognizing the little things about each other anymore that it seemed strange to hear him acknowledge something like that. "I have clients this morning, but call me and let me know what's going on with you. Bye." She did not remember the last time she heard such emotion in his voice. She had worried him. Not enough to stop everything, but he did attempt to reach her.

A second message on her phone was a text from a new number, and she knew it was Knox.

Now you have my number. Call me soon.

It was vague and somewhat safe, in case it had been intercepted by someone else. That consequently caused Afton to feel a wave of guilt inside. *Was this what cheating felt like?* Both anxiety and a rush of something overwhelmingly addictive. Like a drug, she wanted to feel that high from this. She needed to see Knox Manning again. And soon.

Afton Drury was not a bold woman. But she was embracing this change in her. She texted Knox back immediately. And certainly before she lost the nerve to do so.

Share your address with me. And invite me over for dinner sometime soon.

His reply was instant.

537 Holly Avenue. Tonight at 6?

She exhaled.

I will be there. What can I bring?

If only she could have seen the smile on his face when he texted his reply.

Just the woman I cannot stop thinking about.

Afton stored his phone number in her contact list. She thought about deleting their messages, but why? No one ever saw her phone or pried in her life like that. She was boring. She was predictable. Or, at least, she had been.

And then she remembered she needed to let her husband know she was safe. The text she sent to him was, *Got up early to take a walk in the park. I need to start taking better care of me.*

And that was not a lie.

Afton went to the studio to edit the photographs from the wedding in the park. It was getting close to five o'clock when she left for home. She arrived at an empty house again, and quickly changed her clothes. She matched her bra with her panties for the first time in forever. Both were black lace and now underneath a sleeveless mauve sundress. She wore her favorite low-heeled nude sandals.

Ten minutes before six o'clock, she sent her husband a text message before she left their house.

Taking care of Bella tonight for Skye. Probably will be late.

But that was a lie.

As she drove through the historic neighborhood of Saint Paul, she was in awe of it. She had never taken in that rich history before. And when she reached Knox's address, she was eager to see the inside of that folk-style home.

He met her at the door and stepped back for her to come inside. And when she did, she sighed. "This is amazing. The history and the stories inside these walls take away my breath." He smiled so wide his face hurt. They shared that same appreciation.

"That's exactly why I was drawn to this place, and wanted to live in this part of Saint Paul. I'm glad you like it. I want to show you the rest of the house." And he did. She was given the grand tour of every room, every closet, and even the secret staircase that she admitted would probably haunt her in her dreams, and he laughed out loud at her silly side.

They were standing in his bedroom last, and she admired the fireplace. The air conditioner was running in the house, but she wondered how a fire would look in that room regardless of the heat it would generate. It was simply romantic.

"What are you thinking?" he asked her, stepping a little closer to her, but he had not touched her yet.

"I'm thinking you brought me up here to your bedroom lastly on the tour because you have an ulterior motive to keep me here."

He laughed again, but wanted her to know she wasn't exactly correct. "We can take this slow, you know, and just enjoy getting to know each other." He knew she was fragile in many ways. Her marriage had sucked so much life out of her. He wanted to give passion back to her, if she would let him. Or if she had truly never felt swept up in it, then he wanted to be the first to show her. Saying all of that to her would only overwhelm her though.

"I'd like that," she told him, and he led her downstairs for dinner.

He grilled fillets and served those with wild rice and a tossed vinaigrette salad. It was a light and refreshing meal, and perfect for a summer evening.

"You are a wonderful cook," she complimented him as she sipped a glass of white wine. He was having one, too.

"Thank you. I don't cook much at all anymore, not just for myself, so I enjoyed preparing this for us tonight." She smiled. "This is weird for you, isn't it?" He sensed how awkward she felt being there with him, alone in his home.

"We are not really an us," she told him. "I am married and I am having a secret dinner with another man. I want to get to know you, but that feels wrong on so many levels. And what feels even more wrong is wanting you to take me upstairs."

"Your direct honesty is one of the most refreshing things I've ever been on the receiving end of in my entire life," he told her, and she smiled. He did, however, want there to be more than just sex between them.

"I'm not always like this. It's you. It's this new me, with you," she added. "I don't want to think or analyze. I just want to feel." He reached for her hand across the table. This was the first time they had touched since being in the park together this morning.

She closed her eyes for a moment. She willed herself to get lost in this. In him. This new desire was clouding her entire being — all of her thoughts, and her ability to ration those thoughts. Her emotions were completely out of control.

"Afton, I want to be with you, too," he told her. "On your terms though. If we go upstairs and you want to stop what we start, it's okay to tell me that. You can trust that I will respect you and your body." For Knox, being with her already felt like more than just a woman to have sex with. He wanted to get to know her soul as well. Whether she felt the same way, or not, was lost to him still. Because it was too soon. Because she was married and perhaps reeling from the recent realization that her husband was cheating on her with a friend. He was thinking too much, so he stopped himself.

"Thank you," she said to him first. "Take me upstairs. Please." *Before she lost her will... or came to her senses. She was well aware how this was entirely out of character for her.*

He led her by the hand until they reached his bedroom. He left her standing in the middle of the room while he walked over to the fireplace against the far wall. As if he could read her mind, he turned the key on the floor to gas-light a fire. He walked back to her, still standing in the middle of his bedroom. The wall that faced the back of the house was mostly all windows, and just sheer curtains covered them. The only light in the room now was from the fire and the moon shining in the sky directly outside. He touched her cheek with an open palm and she closed her eyes for a moment. She wanted to allow herself to feel this. His lips slowly met hers. There, again, was that endearing gentleness. His lips, his tongue. Her willingness to meet him halfway. They kissed for a long time, and then his hands moved from her face to her nape and then onto her bare shoulders. Her full breasts were pressed against his chest. She could feel the hardness of his desire through the dress shorts he wore. He pressed himself into her lower belly and she moaned. He kissed her hard and full on the mouth this time. "I want you to take off my dress," she told him and turned around for him to unzip it all the way down her back. He did as she asked and then let it fall to the floor. She stood there in her low heels, bra and panties. She felt self-conscious. Her body wasn't what it used to be. And he sensed that hesitation from her. So he lifted her chin and looked into her eyes. "You are so beautiful. Let me make love to you and show you how desirable you are." And, that, was what she wanted most right now.

She reached for the buttons on his shirt and undid them. His shirt joined her dress in a pile on the floor. Next, she unfastened his shorts, and this time he closed his eyes and inhaled a deep breath. His body was so sculptured. So perfect in Afton's eyes. He was younger. And fit. But, any insecurities disappeared the moment he led her over to his bed. She removed her sandals. He took off his shorts. And then he laid her down on the bed, and moved beside her. He kissed her tenderly on the mouth and traced his hands over the lace of her bra. Her nipples reacted. She reached back and undid the clasp of it. Her full breasts sprang free and he touched her first with his fingers. And then he sucked her nipples, one and then the other, until she was panting beneath him. She wanted to reach for him, his manhood. And when she slid her hand inside of his fitted boxer briefs, he groaned. "You first," he said to her hoarsely. "I want this to be about you."

She obliged, because God almighty she wanted that so very much. She wanted to keep feeling like this. Wanting this. Wanting him. That was the sole reason why she was there tonight.

He found the v between her legs. He helped her out of those lacy panties. She was throbbing beneath his touch. He pleasured her with his fingers. She was trembling. "Afton? Is this alright with you?"

"Yes... please don't judge me... but I've never," she paused. *Did she really admit to him that she had never experienced a true orgasm?*

"It's okay..." he told her. "I want to do that for you. Just relax. Your body wants this release. Just let it happen. Don't think, just feel. Well, you can think naughty thoughts to get your mind worked up as well. Never hurts," he teased her and she giggled. It was a hoarse, sexy laugh that turned him on further. He found her again and asked her to part her legs further. She relaxed and he was slowly finding his fingers wet to his touch. He felt her sudden, repetitive throbs as he gently and then more aggressively rubbed over her most sensitive area. When her breathing became rapid, he put his mouth on her. He licked and he sucked until she was almost there. He slid his fingers inside of her and thumbed her clitoris at the same time. She found her rhythm, lost her mind in this fantasy, and he never stopped until she exploded at his fingertips. He again put his mouth on her, down there, and savored what he had done to her body. Her release turned him on more than he could ever remember in his life. She held his face in both of her hands as he crawled his way up her body. He touched her breasts and squeezed the fullness in his grip. "Good for you?" he asked her about *what she claimed was* her very first real orgasm.

"God yes," she admitted, feeling slightly self-conscious for losing such control of herself. But a side of her, that even she was unfamiliar with, had surfaced. And remained still. "I want more of you now. I need to see you enjoying this too." She got him out of his underwear while she spoke.

"Oh I am, believe me," he told her, and she saw the longing in his eyes. She stroked him now, the full length of him, and he spoke out her name. His voice was raspy. "I want to be inside of you." She watched him reach for a foil packet on the nightstand, and then he rolled a condom over himself. College was the last time in her life she had practiced safe sex. And she assumed it had been a long time for Knox as well, considering he and his ex-wife had tried unsuccessfully for a baby.

She spread her legs for him.

He eased himself up to her opening, and slowly entered. "You are so tight," he was surprised to hear himself say.

"I'm sorry," she stated.

"Don't be. You're perfect." He was gentle as he pushed his way deeper inside of her. She arched her back, and gave him unspoken permission to take her all the way. No holding back.

And he didn't resist doing this to her. And with her.

Knox found his rhythm and plunged further and harder as he shifted his hips faster. She grabbed his firm buttocks and he rode her until he could hardly take it anymore. But he wanted more. More time to do this with her until his release.

"God yes," he heard her moan.

"I know," he said in return.

He thumbed the throbbing knob above her entrance again. Her breathing changed quicker this time. She knew what she wanted to feel again. And Knox wanted to come together with her. This time he brought her faster to the edge and when she screamed out in release, he finally joined her.

He was still inside of her as they panted together, and came down from their shared ecstasy. He couldn't speak for her, but he knew after this moment his world would never be the same if she weren't in it.

They shared silence for awhile as he disposed of the protection they had used and then laid naked beside her. Knox propped himself on one elbow, leaned into her and traced her naked body with his fingers. Her perky breasts were his favorite thing in the world right now. "How are you?" he asked her.

"I feel so many things right now," she admitted. "I feel foolish for never having allowed myself to completely enjoy this before. Our bodies can do amazing things. Thank you for showing me how it can be."

"It was my pleasure," he grinned, and she suppressed a giggle. "I'm glad you're okay." He was concerned she would have regrets.

"Knox," she said his name, and he thought he did hear some remorse this time. "I can't stay with you tonight. I—"

"I understand." He wasn't going to make her say it. She had a home —and a husband— to return to. For now.

"Did you want dessert before you have to leave?" he offered, thinking she may have worked up an appetite as he had. "I don't bake or anything, but I do have ice cream."

She smiled and touched his face with her fingertips. He wanted to nurture her and take care of her. That was simply sweet. And truly something new to her. "What I want is you. One more time." He lunged toward her and found his mouth on hers, their tongues intertwined instantly as if they had kissed and been comfortable lovers for years on end.

"You're going to be sore tomorrow," he warned her as his fingers found her willing core again.

"I don't care," she uttered as she succumbed to his touch, down there, once more. And this time was even better than the previous. When she regained her composure, she moved onto her knees in front of him. "Take me from behind." She had done it only once before, and didn't like how uncomfortable she felt. This time, she trusted it would be different and better. And, at the hands of this man who was now her secret lover, it most certainly was.

Chapter 9

It was thirty minutes before midnight when Afton returned home. She thought for a moment, as she entered the kitchen from the garage, that she might have to explain why she had worn a dress just to babysit her niece, if Sam was still awake and had noticed. *Who was she kidding? He never noticed those things anymore.*

She walked through the living room. This sort of felt like a walk of shame to her, only nobody was watching. The stairway lights had allowed her to see her path in the dark room. She noticed two throw pillows out of place on the end of the sofa. She put them back where she liked them, where they belonged. It was as if by arranging those details, she could set the world right again. This was her world, in this house. The home she shared with Sam, the roof and walls that kept them safe as they raised their children year after passing year. She was in the comfort and familiar surroundings of her own home again. She had lost a part of herself tonight when she willingly turned her back on her morals and values. She hadn't let Knox see her come down from the high they shared together, but it started to happen when she was putting clothes back on the body she shared with and had completely given to another man. *How could something feel both wrong and liberating at the very same time?*

In the shower, she lathered up a wash cloth with a bar of soap. And she washed all of the tender places Knox had been. She was raw and sore, and she felt a wave of guilt again when she justified it as *a good hurt* in her mind.

When she slipped into the familiar bed she shared with her husband, he was asleep on his far side of the king-size mattress. She laid there awake for the longest time, on her back, staring upward in the dark, at the high ceiling. Her last thoughts, before she finally drifted off to sleep in the wee hours of the morning, were, *she was a changed woman with absolutely no idea how Knox Manning was going to fit into her world.*

The following morning was much of the same for Afton and Sam's routine. She made coffee and drank hers alone. He came downstairs in time to make a piece of toast and pour a cup of coffee to-go. Afton found herself feeling self-conscious around him, wearing her robe with very little underneath. Her body felt different to her now. It was as if she was aware of it again. And she wondered if Sam would be able to see that change. He hadn't.

During their brief exchange of words, she lied to him twice. He asked about her night with the baby and she had responded it was special one-on-one time with her niece. And when he asked where Skye had gone, she told him on a date. There was no reason for Sam not to believe her.

And Afton believed that was the end of having to fabricate a story to cover up where she had really been last night. Until Skye stormed into her studio a couple hours later.

"What the hell is going on with you?" her youngest sister didn't know how to keep her voice down. She lived life out loud and did not apologize for it. Afton was grateful not to be with a client when she was on the receiving end of a *Skye outburst* that both confused and annoyed her.

"Do you want to tell me what has you so riled already this morning?" Afton rolled her chair back from behind her computer and stood up. Skye had already rushed all the way from the entrance to merely feet away from Afton.

"I dropped off Bella at daycare and went to the gas station. I ran into Sam there. He wanted to know how my date was last night." Afton's face fell. "Yeah. You lied to him. Your husband, for some reason, thinks that you spent half the night babysitting your niece, when you and I both know that's false."

Afton felt her face flush. "What did you tell him?"

"I played along once I realized that I needed to in order to save your ass for something I know nothing about," Skye explained.

"Oh thank God, and thank you," Afton released an obvious sigh of relief.

"Where were you?" A part of Skye was worried. This behavior was unlike her oldest sister. She was the good girl. The good wife. She had never known her to make a bad decision. Ever.

"I know you deserve the truth," Afton began, "but first you have to promise me that you will not tell anyone. Not even Laney. Not yet. I'm just not ready to explain myself."

"Okay you are really scaring me now," Skye admitted. "Are you in some kind of trouble?"

"That depends on how you look at it," Afton actually rolled her eyes at herself. "First, I want to tell you that I discovered Sam is sleeping with Jess Robertson."

Skye's jaw literally dropped. "What? She's your friend! Damn it. I told you he had to be cheating on you. No sex at home and it's a given that any man will go looking for it. But with Jess? How could she do that to you?"

"Exactly my thoughts, thank you," Afton stated.

"So were you following them last night and that's where you were, so you fed Sam the babysitting lie?"

"No, that wasn't last night," Afton told her. "Last night I had dinner with a surgeon from Minneapolis who is recently divorced and he just moved to Saint Paul."

"You had a date? As in, in a public place?" Afton stared at her youngest sister. She owned and operated a website design business. She did most of her work out of her home. She stood in Afton's studio wearing cropped denim that frayed unevenly overtop her shapely calves, with a short t-shirt that showed off her flat belly. Her long blonde hair was pulled up high on her head in a messy bun. At forty years old, she still looked youthful. She, of all people, would understand what Afton did last night.

"I was at his home, Skye."

"Why?" she was seriously confused.

"Because I am attracted to him."

"You're what? But you hate sex. You've said so yourself. Was this date some sort of payback to Sam?" And that was a legitimate question.

"Sam doesn't know that I'm aware of him and Jess. I don't know if a part of me wanted to cheat on him because he's doing it to me. All I know is, for the first time in my life I let myself feel desired, and it was wonderful."

"You had sex with a stranger?"

"He's not exactly a stranger to me."

"Do you even hear yourself?" Skye raised her voice and scolded Afton, probably for the very first time ever in their lives. There had never been a reason to before. Afton was the good sister. The one who avoided conflict and always proceeded with caution. "Are you having some sort of mid-life crisis?"

"Stop yelling, and please don't try to analyze me," she paused before she said what came naturally to say next. "I'll admit, I am carrying some guilt over this."

"Was it just a one-night-stand, you think?" Skye forced herself to calmly speak.

"He wants to see me again."

"And how do you feel about that?"

"Conflicted," Afton was out-loud-honest for the first time right now with both Skye and herself.

"Oh boy," Skye replied and her tone sounded worried for her sister. "This isn't going to end well. You used a man for sex and now he wants a relationship. Those types are hard to shake." Skye would know.

"I feel terrible even thinking that there is any truth to what you just said."

"What does that even mean?" Skye asked her. "You can't seriously think that you are going to be able to date another man, or take a lover as you seem to see it, while you're married to Sam? You're not dishonest enough to sneak around. It's not how you are designed."

Afton put her face in her hands for a moment. "I need to figure this out."

"There's nothing to figure out. Just stop seeing him, or screwing him!"

"Whose side are you on anyway?" Afton called her out.

"You know I'm not a Sam fan."

"Then support me. Give me the time I need to figure this out, and just be my listening ear when I can't make sense of what I've let happen. Or the fact that I just might not want to stop. Not yet anyway."

"What have you done with my sister?" Skye asked her. The change in Afton was noticeable to her, and for Skye it was really difficult to grasp.

"I'm a woman, too," Afton said, suddenly sounding more like her wiser self again.

"That's fair," Skye relented. "Just be careful. Call me anytime, okay? I'm here for you." For the first time since Afton felt as if her life was beginning to unravel, starting with seeing Sam and Jess together, she felt emotional. The tears in her eyes caught her entirely off guard. She was not a crier. *She hated to cry!* Skye reacted by pulling her into the kind of close, comforting hug Afton hadn't realize how much she needed.

Chapter 10

Before noon, Afton received a text message from Knox. Her heart rate quickened and she felt her body temperature rise. She wasn't exactly sure what she should say to him.

Can we get the awkward out of the way and meet for lunch?

Afton stared at his message for awhile before she set her phone down and thought about what to say to him. She didn't want to meet for lunch. Her stomach was in knots as it was, and food wouldn't help. Running from, or ignoring him, wasn't the answer either. Finally, Afton responded.

We should talk. Mears Park? Our bench?

After she sent the message, she cringed a bit. They weren't a couple who shared things like a particular bench in the park. She was, again, misleading him. Afton only wished she knew at this point exactly what she was doing. She should have ceased communication with him, or just disregarded his attempt to reach out to her. Instead, she had agreed to meet Knox in person. She felt herself falling into that trap again. And the confusing part about it was she wanted to be there.

Knox was waiting for her when she walked a portion of the trail to reach the park bench. It was midday and there were not many people around. For that, Afton was thankful, as she felt like she was doing something wrong. One look from anyone else, and they would recognize the obvious.

He stood as she reached him. Afton noticed he wore shorts that showed off his great legs, and a t-shirt that form-fitted his torso. "Hi," she said first.

Knox smiled. "You look beautiful," he told her, and she immediately felt uncomfortable. She was wearing a black, sleeveless shift dress and silver flip flops on her feet. She wasn't accustomed to feeling beautiful, or being told so. Her expression told him that he should scale back a notch, or five, with the compliments.

"I want to be fair to you," Afton said, outright, as they both sat down. Knox stayed silent and listened. "Last night was so out of character for me, as I know you understand that. And today, it's all about guilt and shame for me." She wanted to fix this, but she couldn't erase what happened, or ignore the fact that she was the one who wanted him. She initiated how fast they progressed. She downright begged if she really thought about it.

'That's not only understandable, but it's expected," Knox stated. They weren't sitting too close, and he never made any attempt to touch her. "What happened between us, happened fast, and taking a step back might be a good idea to allow yourself to regroup. That's why I wanted to meet with you today. I don't want you to panic and run away. Just be open with me about how you feel."

71

Afton turned her body inward on the bench, so she could sit sideways and look at him, really look at him. He was younger than her, and starting his life over. He should be looking for a woman who could give him a baby. Not a woman like her, who was older and obviously on the brink of having some sort of mid-life crisis. "Why do you have to be so good, and compliant with my confusion and uncertainty?"

He smiled. "It's easy with you. You have an honest heart and you want to do the right thing, but there's a side of you that's just done with going along with that. That woman emerges when we are together, and I don't just mean in the physical sense. Just listening to you speak, reveals so much. It might be time for you to pay attention to that woman inside of you who is trying to emerge."

"I wish I understood myself as well as you seem to think you get me."

"I'm not going anywhere, Afton. Take all the time you need. But don't shut me out. This bench. Or my place. I want to help you figure this out."

"Why?" Afton asked him. "I came here thinking we could call it a one-time thing."

"And I still hope that will not be the case. It's your call, Afton."

"But I'm married..." she heard herself say.

"Right," Knox paused before he continued. "To a man who is not being faithful to you." He refrained from mentioning their lack of communication and intimacy. That was between Afton and her husband.

And now, that person was Afton as well. *The unfaithful spouse.* Sam may have been able to live with himself, but Afton was not so sure she could do the same.

One day later, Skye stepped off the elevator at Regency Minneapolis Hospital. She wore two-and-a-half-inch navy blue heels and a white blouse with an oversized collar that was unbuttoned conservatively on her chest. As cheesy as it sounded in her head, today she was *dressed for success* to attend a meeting with the hospital's public relations director. Skye was there to pitch what she could offer them as their website designer. The hospital was looking for something new and innovative and Skye was confident she would be hired, despite the fact that she heard two other companies were vying for the job. She carried a rectangular-shaped bag on her shoulder, storing her laptop. And when she turned the next corner too short, that bag and her entire shoulder collided with an oncoming person.

"Oh!" Skye reacted, in her typical loud manner. She didn't have an inside voice.

"It's fine. Probably just as much my fault," the attractive male in front of her spoke. In heels, at already five-eight, Skye nearly matched his six-foot height. His face was tan and his brownish, probably more blond hair, was borderline in need of a trim. It wasn't unkempt, just a little wild. He wore a white lab coat, as had every other person Skye already met in those hospital halls. But she hadn't nearly knocked them down.

She regrouped, moving the wide strap of her bag back onto her shoulder. And then she suppressed a giggle.

"What's funny?" he asked, because it was just human nature to want to know.

Skye sized him up in his white-collared dress shirt and navy-blue pants. He also wore brown dress shoes on his feet. "You got the memo," she held up both her hands and pointed back to her own outfit.

"Ah, same colors. Great minds…" he started to say, and she knew the rest.

"Right," she nodded, and smiled. He was boyishly handsome, and Skye was never one to shy away from flirting. "Doctor… Manning," she added with a delay as she took the time to read the personalized stitching above the left breast pocket of his lab coat.

"Yes, Knox Manning." For a moment, Knox wondered why he stated his first name. It was his first day back after a five-week leave of absence. He wasn't in the groove yet. And she was a beautiful woman — with legs up to her neck. The short-enough skirt she wore enhanced that incredible feature. "And you are?"

"Skye Gallant." He smiled. The unique named appeared to match the woman. "So, Dr. Knox… what do you specialize in?" That question could have been perceived as entirely inappropriate.

"Orthopedics," he answered. "And what about yourself?"

"Web design. I'm meeting with the PR director."

"So Regency could be a potential new client for you?" Knox was a little impressed by a woman who knew technology.

"That's the plan," she smiled.

"Well, much luck to you," Knox offered, and began to move away from her.

"I appreciate that," Skye replied as they parted ways. And before she stepped further in the opposite direction, she glanced back at Dr. Manning. If Skye had bumped into him anywhere else… she would not have let him get away so quickly.

Skye left that meeting with a good feeling. She believed she succeeded at delivering her pitch for Regency Minneapolis to hire her to revamp their website. She worked on their potential site for weeks, and the end result showed. Her presentation had impressed PR Director Jamie Block, who had all but hired Skye on the spot. *Skye would be hearing from them soon.*

She had to control the spring in her step as she walked the long corridor back to the elevator. She didn't know her way around that facility very well, so she backtracked her steps to find her way out. She spotted that same elevator in the distance and made her way to it. When she pressed the lower level button on the wall, the doors opened in front of her. And she was again face-to-face with Knox Manning.

"Dr. Knox, we meet again," she smiled, and he chuckled under his breath at her greeting.

"I'm judging by your disposition that the meeting must have gone well?"

"I'm hopeful, yes," Skye stated, trying not to boast about her confidence and her capabilities as a professional.

"Well good," Knox smiled. "I'm sure Jamie Block knows when not to let something beneficial get away."

She certainly hoped so. "How about you?" Skye asked him.

"Me?"

"Do you know when not to let something, or someone, slip through your fingers?"

For a fleeting moment, Knox thought of Afton. *He's been there.* "I guess I do, yes," he answered her.

"Then how about a drink sometime? My treat." Skye was bold and coy, and she made no apologies for it. Not even in a professional environment.

"You're asking me out?" Knox kept his voice low, as he had stepped off the elevator and the door closed behind his back. He wasn't ready to put her on there and have her get away. He, again, thought of Afton. He reminded himself that he was a patient man, and he told her he would wait for her. But then there was this woman with those legs and that personality that just wouldn't quit, awaiting his answer. *One drink,* he thought.

"I am," Skye spoke up.

"My shift ends at 5. We could meet at Up-Down." It was a roomy, watering hole on Lyndale that Skye had frequented a few times. It still had the old-school pinball and video games, as she recalled playing a few rounds of each with a date who had turned out to be more like a buddy.

Skye's first thought was that five o'clock was early for her, but she would arrange for a babysitter to make this happen. After all, she initiated it. "Plan on it," she told him.

As they parted, they never exchanged phone numbers. Somehow, they both trusted the other one would be there.

Chapter 11

Skye's cellphone rang just as she pulled into the parking lot at Up-Down. She whipped her jeep into the nearest parking spot. Afton was calling her.

"Hey Aft, what's going on?" It was a rarity for them to talk as often as they had the past few days. Considering what Afton was going through, Skye was quick to take her call.

"I met with him today in the park," she admitted. And she felt relieved to have someone else to talk to about this drama that she had brought into her life.

"The guy you slept with?"

"Jesus Skye, keep your voice down. Where are you?"

"In my jeep, in a parking lot. No one can hear me. Chill the hell out."

Afton smiled a little on the opposite end of the phone. She did need to calm down. "Yes, him. We talked. He said he will be patient with me as I attempt to sort out this confusion in my brain."

"Sounds fair if you were single. Afton, seriously, break it off before you get caught. Unless you plan to divorce Sam?"

That thought had not entered her mind. Not yet. "No," she was quick to answer. "I am torn. I enjoy his company. He talks to me for chrissakes. And, just as wonderful, he listens."

"He just wants in your pants, Aft. All men are like that."

"Maybe so, but he's not pressuring me. And I just need time to think."

"Then think. Keep me posted on those thoughts too." Skye glanced at the clock in her jeep. It was 4:58. "Listen, I am about to get out and go in—" Her phone cut out and Afton missed what she said.

"Where are you and Bella going?"

"Bella is at home with our teenage neighbor. I am at Up-Down, meeting someone for a drink."

That was nothing new. "Someone new?" Afton asked. Maybe a part of her, for the first time ever, envied her little sister. *She was free to date. And sleep around.* Afton embarrassed herself with that thought.

"Actually yes. A medical doctor that I just met today. Long story, but I was working, had a meeting, and literally bumped into him. He's really hot."

Afton nearly rolled her eyes, but she didn't. "Go. Have fun."

79

"Talk to you soon, okay?" Skye wanted to be sure Afton knew she had an open invitation to stay in touch. And a part of Skye so badly wanted to confide in their other sister. Laney would be shocked to know what was happening with Afton.

She walked into the bar, right on time. And she was quick to spot Knox, waiting for her, bar side. He had not changed clothes. *He looked dapper in those navy pants and white dress shirt.* She had worn a slightly-ruffled-hemmed short white skirt with a black blouse that had a scoop-neck low enough to reveal the top of her cleavage. She looked sexy. And Knox caught himself wanting to see her legs again and he was pleased she had worn another skirt to show them off. He was attracted to her, no doubt. But he cared about Afton, and he had not been able to ignore the way guilt panged his chest.

"Dr. Knox," she smiled as her nickname for him so easily rolled off her tongue.

"Good to see you made it, Skye Gallant." She sat down beside him. When he turned to look at her closer, he noticed the fine patch of freckles across the bridge of her nose that makeup didn't entirely conceal, up close. He felt a little taken aback. As if this was a blatant reminder to him that Afton was still on the verge of choosing to explore a relationship with him.

She noticed him staring. "Something wrong?"

"No. Not at all. What would you like to drink?" He already had a beer on the bar top in front of him.

"I thought this was my treat?" she partly teased him, and then told the bartender who approached them that she wanted a vodka tonic.

"Please. The gentleman in me couldn't handle that."

The conversation and the flirting continued for three hours. They ordered a pizza from the grill and more drinks as the night went on. The thing that had intrigued Knox the most about her was that she was a single mother, by choice. Skye was a little annoyed by all of his baby questions, until he confided in her how his marriage had recently ended in divorce because he and his wife were not able to conceive. That fact certainly humanized the man she was first drawn to because of his beautiful face and flawless body.

Knox watched her glance at her phone, which he assumed was either for the time or to check her messages. *She had a baby waiting for her at home.*

"You need to get going," he stated, as if he was looking out for her now.

"Why did the fact that I have a child turn you off?" Skye asked him outright.

Did it seem that way? "I don't mean for it to appear that way. Skye, you're a beautiful woman. And I'm attracted to you. But,"

She placed her hand in his upper thigh and slid it inward. He tightened. "You could follow me home. I'll pay the sitter. Stay with me for awhile?"

"No strings? Just sex?" he asked her. It was easy to be outright with her. And he believed he knew what she wanted. She was an independent, perhaps lonely woman, who didn't need a permanent man. Just an occasional one.

"You're a quick learner," she said, and stood first. "I'm going home." Knox knew it was now or never with this woman. If it wasn't going to be him, it would be someone else. He had nothing to lose. He was, after all, a single man. *With Afton in waiting. Or at least, he had said he was waiting for her.* He threw a wad of cash on the bar.

And then he followed her home.

He waited while Skye paid the babysitter, who appeared to be a responsible teenager who reacted as if she was a little embarrassed to see him, a stranger, in Skye's house. The two-story house was immense for a single mother. It was obvious to him that Skye had done well for herself. He never looked around too much. He did see a few baby pictures, from a safe distance, in the living room, but he didn't want to be weird and stare. Or attempt to get to know her better. She only wanted this to be about hooking up tonight. And so did he.

Skye locked the front door and dimmed the living room lights. She asked him to wait while she checked on her sleeping baby upstairs. When she returned, Knox was seated on the end of her ivory-colored leather sofa. "Can I get you a drink? she asked, standing toe to toe with him. He reached for her hand. It was the first time he had done that all night. And then he pulled her down on his lap. He initiated their kiss, and Skye quickly escalated it. She was eager, and Knox could tell this was going to happen right there if they didn't slow down. *But who said anything about slowing down?*

She felt his hands on her chest. He moved them up her shirt and ran his fingers over her lacy bra. She helped herself out of that shirt for him. And then she watched him take off his. She touched his firm chest and ran her fingernails down to his belt. He allowed her to undo it. She wasn't a patient woman, and he enjoyed that about her. He lifted her skirt above her hips. He found her core through more lace, and then pushed that material aside. Two of his fingers teased her tender folds, and entered her. She moaned. He tightened. Her bra came off at Skye's doing. He pressed his mouth to her nipples and nearly lost his mind indulging in a woman with no expectations other than this, what they were doing right now. Not once had he thought of Afton since he had walked inside of Skye's home. This was all about a booty call. She maneuvered off her skirt. And he helped her remove her panties along with it. He dropped his pants and underwear, and she straddled him. She reached for him, his full length, and he held his breath. There was a condom from his wallet on the sofa next to them. She rolled it over him. It was seductive to have her do it. He reacted and kissed her hard on the mouth. Grabbed her breasts with both of his hands. And then he moved a hand between her legs. She was ready and he teased her. "Now, Knox. Make me lose control."

She knelt. He moved down between her open legs to meet his mouth to her. She practically rode his tongue, her legs were shaky when she finally exploded into his mouth. He couldn't wait much longer to be inside her. She sensed that and quickly straddled him, bringing his full length to her opening. He pushed himself in. Abruptly. She gasped. And then she took control and moved her hips over him. He was close. So damn close. She was in control and he liked it. But at the last minute, he lifted her up and off of him. He stood, bent her over the sofa, and took her from behind. He humped her hard. Again. And again. He felt his full length reach far inside, and another thrust later he heard her cry out again just as he too came. She fell forward on the sofa, and he remained standing. "Be right back," he said, as he escaped to dispose of the protection he had used. When he returned, naked and still reeling from the satisfaction they shared, he found her partially dressed again with her skirt and bra back on.

Her messaged was received loud and clear. *It was time for him to go.*

He reached down on the floor for his pants and he felt rushed to put them back on. All the while, they shared silence.

"You want me to go, don't you?" Knox knew.

She nodded, almost as if she was timid, or ashamed. And that was not the woman he had been with tonight.

Skye oddly looked away as he finished dressing himself. When Knox was ready, he felt disheveled and far from put together, as she walked with him over to the front door and unlocked it. Again, neither of them had asked each other for a phone number, or anything more. And Knox was not about to mention the prospect of seeing her again.

But little did he know, there was a photograph on the sofa table behind them tonight. It was a fairly recent capture of Skye with her sisters. And Afton was in the middle.

Chapter 12

There was both shame and liberation in how he felt. He had a one-night stand. Knox hadn't been that careless since he was in college. He didn't count Afton, because he wanted to see her again, and he had.

Knox stepped out of the shower, wrapped a towel around his middle, and walked into his bedroom. He stood in front of the fireplace he had lit because it was raining outside and he felt chilled when he entered his house with the air conditioner running. He thought of being in his bedroom with Afton, and how sharing a romantic fire with her had meant something. *Their getting together had meant something to him.* Tonight was just sex. He and a beautiful woman named Skye only used each other for their bodies. Knox knew he would never do something that mindless again. Even though he was a more-than-willing participant, he still felt used. And ashamed. He wanted more for himself. He wanted a relationship, a woman to make love to in his bed, and to hold afterward. He wanted Afton.

He turned away from the fire and walked over to the nightstand beside his bed. It was late, but he felt compelled to reach out to her.

The text message he sent was, *I want to build something more with you. Take that chance with me.*

Afton had not seen the text from Knox until the next morning. It strangely had brought a smile to her face, and a flutter in her belly. Her life, which had become typical and mundane after their children moved out on their own, was now complicated. She had taken a huge risk when she got involved with another man. And day by day since, Afton had mixed emotions concerning what she should do now. Ending it, labeling what they shared as just a one-time-thing, seemed to be the most sensible choice. But there was something about Knox that tugged at her heart the first time she met him, and especially the more she got to know him. And he wanted her to choose him. There was a lot at stake here. Her entire life was on the line. If Afton had that kind of courage —to start something new from the ground up, to take a chance on uncertainty— she never knew it.

Afton stood facing the counter and the cornered windows over the sink as she sipped the hot coffee. Her back was to Sam when he walked in. He didn't want to startle her with his voice, so he cleared his throat first. She turned around immediately.

"I didn't hear you come in." Typically, she heard his dress shoes on the hardwood flooring once he descended the steps. She looked down at the black dress socks on his feet. He wasn't completely ready to go out the door for work.

"I think you should sit down," he told her, unexpectedly.

"What's going on?" She instantly felt unsettled, and she ignored his suggestion for her to sit. Whatever he had to tell her, she would take standing up. Her first thought was Sam was leaving her. He would want a divorce to free himself to be with Jess. Afton couldn't help herself. She then imagined the chance to pursue whatever she and Knox had between them. She would just go for it. No more wavering her thoughts and giving in to reservations about Knox being younger and not yet having lived through some of the things she had. Namely, having and raising children of his own.

Sam had mistaken her distraction for worry. "I don't know how to tell you this, other than to just say it." Afton already set her coffee mug down on the counter. Her freed hands were trembling a little, so she put them in the pockets of her terrycloth robe. She knew what he had to say was going to be life changing. "Mark had a heart attack in the shower this morning. He's dead."

Afton covered her mouth with her hand. It was a gesture of shock, and being utterly speechless. "No…" was her first response and it sounded more like a whimper than a word. Tears sprung to her eyes. *She hated to cry!*

"I know," Sam said, and he rubbed her shoulder, back and forth, several times. It was both a strange and a familiar comfort to have him touch her again. "I'm canceling my morning clients. I think we should go to Jess, you know, to the house to offer our support."

Sam never missed work. Births. Deaths. Snowstorms. Mudslides. It didn't matter to Sam. Work took precedence. For a moment, Afton pushed her shock and sadness aside, as she felt unnerved by the fact that he wanted to go to Jess. But the reality was, they both should go.

"Was Jess the one who called you?" Afton's phone never rang. She had it right there in the kitchen with her. But Sam was Jess' first choice. Of course he was.

"Yes," he nodded. "She's a wreck. She found him after he was taking too long in the shower."

"How awful," Afton said, and sincerely meant it. Forcing aside her recent hurt and disgust for Jess Robertson, she was devastated for her loss. Mark was a wonderful man. He had a heart of gold. Not only would his family and friends suffer his loss, but the community of Saint Paul as well. Mark dedicated so much of his life to serving the people in that town during their greatest time of need. His compassion for others —for their pain and their grief— had always touched Afton.

Sam stayed silent. Afton watched him pour himself some coffee. He was hurting. He and Mark were friends. Afton had to shove aside the thought of Sam sleeping with Mark's wife. A part of her really wished she hadn't known that disgusting truth.

"I have to blow dry my hair, and throw on some clothes. Will you wait for me?"

"Yes I want to go there together," she heard Sam say to her as she left the kitchen. And Afton didn't ignore the fact that she couldn't remember the last time he said that to her.

She hurried to blow dry her hair, and before she got dressed, she made a phone call to her daughter. Afton wanted her children to hear this devastating news from her. The Robertson family was important to them too.

Amy answered after the second ring. It was early and she was still getting ready for work. At 22 years old, Amy was in her first year working as a dental hygienist for a family-owned practice in Minneapolis.

"Mom? What's wrong?" This wasn't a typical time for a phone conversation about nothing at all.

"Amy, I have some terrible news. Mark Robertson had a massive heart attack this morning and died."

She heard her daughter gasp on the opposite end of the phone. "Oh my gosh, that can't be true... Poor Addi and Spencer, and Jess too. I can't believe this."

"I know. It's awful. Your dad and I are going to their house soon. I just wanted to call you before the word gets out. Let your brother know for me, will you?"

"Of course." They both knew Latch was probably already at the auto body shop where he had been working as a mechanic since he was 16 years old. And that was eight years ago.

Afton had to rush their phone call, but what more could be said? This was a tragedy.

Chapter 13

Afton made her rounds, giving hugs and trying to offer some comfort to Mark and Jess' children, his parents, and even Jess. They all wore faces of shock and disbelief. How could a man —at the helm of their family, and a staple in the community— suddenly just be gone? It was a lot to grasp, and too much to understand. Afton tried to suppress her tears, but just watching all of them had caused her to give in at times.

She felt a collision of mixed emotions, however, when she stood in the background and watched Jess fall into her husband's arms. Sam embraced her, and held her for what seemed like too long. *Had he ever rubbed her back like that and spoke soft, soothing words in her ear? If he had, Afton had long forgotten.* She couldn't help herself. She was unnerved and offended watching them together. Jess was alone now. Available. Ready and waiting for Sam to take a permanent, public place in her life. The prospect of Sam wanting out of their marriage was one thing, but for Afton to think that Jess could bat her eyes or disrobe her body and have him all to herself was another. Again, Afton was more upset with Jess than her own husband over their secret affair. It was strange, but true. And Afton realized it was because she really didn't want Sam anymore. Not in that way. But to know one of her closest friends was sleeping with him was extremely hard for her to accept. But today, she was keeping herself in check. Because Jess was truly grieving the death of her husband. Afton retold that to herself repeatedly. She knew if this had happened to her, regardless of how their relationship had changed and came apart at the seams, she would unravel if Sam died. She forced her compassion to exceed her anger and disappointment. Mark deserved that. He was a good man, and a good friend.

In the car, driving home, they didn't speak. Sometimes Afton didn't mind their shared silence. It was who they were, or who they had become as a couple. But today, knowing where they had been, and feeling certain that Sam had Jess on his mind, there was not a sound as loud as the silence between them.

When they walked into their house together, Sam threw his keys on the table with more force than usual. They hit the surface and bounced off and landed on the floor near the L-shaped island.

Afton only stared at him for a moment before she opted to speak. "Life is fleeting, Sam. We don't know how much time any of us have."

"I know that!" he snapped at her, but then quickly recovered. Sam rarely lost his temper. Afton excused that now, as he was hurting. The shock and the grief yet to come could trigger all kinds of emotion in anyone. "But, a man like Mark? Why him? He had more left to give. His presence was so big in everything he touched. He wasn't just shortchanged of his life, but we all were robbed of having him." It was a wonderful thing to say, as his friend, and Afton was touched. But she also felt like shaking her head and calling him out for his betrayal with his friend's wife.

"I agree," was all she said.

Sam walked over to their stainless steel refrigerator, and opened the door. "Do you want a drink?"

It was noon. Afton smiled a little at him, or maybe just at the thought of day drinking. "Actually, yes, I do."

He never asked what she wanted, he just grabbed two longnecks from the bottom shelf, twisted off the caps of both, and handed her one. Afton rarely drank beer, but Sam had known she did like it. She took a long sip, and then closed her eyes for a moment. Everything about this day, from first thing in the morning, was hard to believe. "I don't know the last time I had a beer," she giggled.

He chuckled, too. "I wondered that after I handed it to you. Something different never hurts anyone."

Afton agreed. "There's going to be a lot of firsts and many changes ahead for Jess and the kids."

"I can't imagine," Sam replied, drinking his beer. They were both seated at the island together now.

"You would manage," she said, knowing he certainly would. He had his career, the kids were independent. And he had Jess. She cringed at that truth.

Sam stared at her for a long time before he spoke. She wondered if he was going to just ignore her comment, until he finally did address it. "I do take for granted that you are always going to be here. It's human nature. You're my wife."

Afton nodded, but she didn't completely agree. What they had done to each other through the years was not human nature. Losing sight of the love and the affection was careless. She knew she was partly responsible, as she had not been interested in being a wife to him in the full sense. They weren't lovers. She thought of Knox. This was the first time since this morning's chaos that her mind had settled. *If she left Sam, for Knox, what would her life be like? At 50 she would be starting over... much like Jess. And who's to say she and Knox would even work out in the end?*

"We become set in our ways, and with much of the same routine day after day," she began. "It just gets comfortable."

Sam nodded, and finished his beer. "That's truly it," he told Afton. "Like an old pair of shoes, or a worn wallet." That analogy offended her. *Did she really want to be compared to something broken in and worn out? Because regardless of its comfort, those kinds of things eventually needed to be parted with, thrown out, and replaced.*

She was done sharing conversation with him. Her bottle of beer was still half full, and she left it on the countertop of the island as she stood. "Are you going to the office today?"

"Soon," he told her.

"Yeah, me too," she stated, but she wondered if he would have even asked her about the rest of her day's plans.

Even sharing an impromptu beer and rare conversation had not changed anything between them. Her husband saw her as someone who would always be there. *Well, damn it. Sometimes, comfortable and predictable didn't make people happy.* And it had taken Afton years to come to terms with that fact.

Losing Mark was unexpected. Yes. Afton's eyes were forced open. But not in the form of appreciating what she already had, and never taking anything or anyone for granted ever again. More like, what else could be attainable for her in this lifetime? While Sam admitted taking his wife and the comfort of their life together for granted —just as he had an old wallet in his ass pocket— Afton was focused on making some changes in her life.

Chapter 14

Mark Robertson's funeral was unbearably sad. He was the third-generation owner and director of the very same funeral home where his family, friends, and the community celebrated him and his life for the final time. It was strange for everyone to be honoring Mark and not to see him walking around there, ensuring that everyone's needs were met. He was always the man in charge in that element. Afton had not recognized the gentleman in a dark suit who was temporarily doing Mark's duties. The blaring truth was, Mark was not coming back and there were a number of blanks that had to be filled in. But everyone knew that no one else could fill his shoes. He couldn't be replaced. At least not in the same, wonderful way.

Their children sat with them in the church pew. Sam was on the end, and Amy was beside him. Afton sat in the middle of her children. Latch wrapped his arm around her a few times to comfort her throughout the memorial service. The music, the words spoken, all were messages of death being so final for everyone left behind on earth. And when Afton dabbed away tears on her face throughout the entire service, she was touched by her son's compassion. He was so unlike his father. Or maybe, he was a replica of Sam in his younger years. She wasn't for certain anymore.

Her sisters had been at the funeral visitation. When the three of them were huddled together, Laney openly cried for her co-worker, Jess. Afton felt Skye staring, as she likely wanted to tell their sister right then and there that Jess had cheated on her beloved, dearly-departed husband with their brother-in-law. Afton avoided making eye contact with Skye when they both listened to Laney express her sorrow.

Following the memorial service, Afton stood in the parking lot of the church with her children and Sam. Latch told them he had to get back to work and was not going to the cemetery or the luncheon that was scheduled at Mark's favorite Italian restaurant in downtown Saint Paul. And Amy also had only taken the morning off from work. Afton hugged them both, and thanked them for being a part of Mark's farewell the past few days. It had been a comfort to Afton, and she assumed for Sam too, to have their children around them.

It was just the two of them again, then. Sam and Afton went together to the cemetery service, pre-burial. And then they joined everyone at the restaurant. There, Afton had spoken to friends she hadn't seen in years, and caught up with a few familiar former Saint Paul residents who had known Mark in school. She did most of this socializing separate from Sam. She noticed, from a distance, that he had stayed close to Mark and Jess' children. And, at times, Jess. They appeared to be caught up in easy conversation. There were no shared glances or touches between them. Jess had played the role well of a grieving widow. And the truth was, Afton believed her sincerity. She just didn't trust the woman with her husband anymore. And she never would again.

When they left the restaurant, Sam told her he was going to bring her home, and then immediately leave for his office. *He had work to catch up on.* Afton thought of Jess. *Was he going to see her? Would she be alone already?* There had been too many relatives and people in and out of the Robertson's home the last few days. Afton doubted her speculation was true. Instead of allowing herself to imagine the worst, she spoke up before he left downtown Saint Paul. "Bring me to the studio instead. I'll get a ride home later."

"You sure?" Sam asked her, before he turned in the opposite direction of their home.

"I am. Thanks."

Afton unlocked the door to her studio that had been closed for a few days. It felt good to be back there. In the silence. The past few days had been consumed with people, and chatter, and memories, and tears. She embraced being alone right now.

She checked her phone for any messages that had gone ignored while she was at the funeral.

One text was from Skye. *Call me sometime soon.*

A missed call was business related, and Afton would return that call today.

And a second text was from Knox. She had explained to him what happened to their good friend, Mark. He offered his sympathy, and reminded her that he wanted to be there for her. Through anything. Afton had refrained from explaining to Knox that their good friend who passed away was the same man whose wife was screwing around with Sam. That detail would be told later. And now, Afton wanted to reply to his text that he had sent several hours ago.

It read: *Thinking of you today. It's never easy to say goodbye to a friend.*

Afton looked at the time. It was 4:45. She assumed Knox would be at the hospital still. She replied to his text.

Your words are a comfort to me. Are you at the hospital right now?

His reply was not instant, but almost thirty minutes later, Afton heard back from him.

I'm glad. Leaving now. Can I see you?

Afton didn't think twice. Probably because she had been thinking about this ever since she told Sam to drop her off at the studio. He wasn't going to be home. There was no plan for dinner as they had both overeaten at Mark's luncheon. She was free.

I need a ride from my studio, but I don't want to go home.

Knox's reply put a much-welcomed smile on her face, and that familiar flutter in her belly again.

Be there in ten minutes.

Knox came into her studio. The closed sign was posted, but the door was unlocked for him.

"Hi there," he said softly, as she walked around her desk and met him in the middle of the room, just as they had the day they first met. "Come here," he said, as he opened his arms to her. And Afton fell into them and cried.

"It's hard, I know. Losing friends in any capacity, through death or just seeing a friendship end, hurts." He held her close and touched her hair. When she pulled back, her face was again wet with tears.

"I'm sorry. I'm really not a crier," she defended her current state of weakness.

"It's okay. You're sad. It's expected."

"He will be sorely missed," she spoke, drying her tears with her fingers.

"How's his family? Does he have children?" Even Knox expected everyone to have children. He knew this businessman was in his mid-fifties and had left behind a wife. There had been some chatter about it at the hospital, as the man was renowned and well-liked in the entire community.

"Yes, two. The same ages as mine. And his wife, Jess is devastated, or at least she puts on an Oscar-worthy performance."

Afton watched him crease his brow a bit. "Were they not close?'

"They were, I think. He adored her, again, I think. We were all friends and had dinner together frequently. You see... my friend, Jess is the woman that my husband has been intimate with."

Knox's eyes widened. "Unbelievable. And that, no doubt, has made the last few days a whirlwind for you."

"To say the least," Afton agreed.

"Do you want to get out of here?" he asked her, on a whim, yet he knew she didn't want to go home just yet.

"Please," she stated.

"My place?" Knox didn't want her to assume anything, but given the fact that she was married, they couldn't just show up anywhere together in public. "We could order takeout, or just talk?"

Afton smiled. She didn't need food, but she did want the comfort of being with him. Wherever that would again lead.

Chapter 15

Afton did change her mind and asked Knox to drive her home, but only to pick up her own vehicle. She then followed him to Holly Avenue. The only time she had ever been in his house seemed like much longer ago than it was. She felt different, changed somehow, since she first came —and left— there. And that feeling didn't have everything to do with being intimate with Knox. It was more about Afton recognizing the fact that she had only one life to live. And it was time she lived it for herself.

She sat down in the middle of his maroon-leather sectional. Knox went into the kitchen and came back with a glass of water for her.

"Cutting me off tonight, are you?" she teased, and he chuckled.

"It's good to have a clear head after the day you've had."

She agreed, and took two sips of the iced water. "You must be starving for dinner, and here I am taking up space on your furniture."

"I'm a big boy. I'll eat when I'm hungry. As for the space you occupy here, I happen to like it. And I could get used to it very quickly."

"I wish I was as certain about life as you are."

"Who says that's true? For years I held onto false hope that my wife would get pregnant and our marriage would survive that strain and everything else until the end of time. I grew tired of feeling certain that would happen, letdown after letdown. Afton, it's when we realize that life is made of uncertainty, that we can finally just let it all go."

"Because we really have no control?"

"Yes and no," he told her. "I believe in taking control of what I want, or need. I just do that now with an open mind that everything has the potential to change."

"The last few days I feel more compelled to embrace change," she admitted, and he watched her take his hand that was between them on the couch cushion. Their fingers intertwined.

"I'm here, when you're ready," he told her, and he truly felt patient. After the one-night stand with Skye Gallant, he had some time to think. He knew what he wanted, and didn't want, for his life now. Talking on the sofa all night long. Holding hands. Sharing hopes and dreams. There were times already when he could see Afton's soul. That meant something to him. While he did desire her body, he truly wanted to capture her heart, too.

"I need to admit something to you," she said, still touching him. "With you, I feel desire that I've never experienced before. The other night, I wanted you. I wanted mind-blowing sex, the kind that my sisters have gloated about. I really thought that chance for me was over, as half of my life is already behind me. You gave me a night to remember, and a part of me thought that's all it was going to be. You have made it very clear that you want more. And I am slowly reaching an understanding with myself that I may just want that, as well. With you."

"Praise God!" Knox teased, and overexaggerated his relief, as she clarified that point.

She giggled. "I don't know what you see in a woman, an older woman when you could have anyone out there." Knox thought of Skye Gallant. He had her, but it wasn't a soul-to-soul connection like he felt with the woman next to him right now.

"I see more than you will ever know. I appreciate everything about you, your mind, your body, your heart and your soul. And I know there's so much more to learn yet." Knox was falling for her, but he kept that revelation to himself still.

"And, when I look at you, I see perfection," Afton told him. "Flawless perfection on the outside. And inside your mind —and your heart— I find myself wanting to hear more of your words, your beliefs, your values, and just the way you view the world. Something was altered inside me when I met you. You have this way of guiding me to my own light that I couldn't find before. I don't even know if I'm making any sense here…"

"What you said was beautiful," he told her. "I know it's too soon, and the last thing I want to do is send you reeling away in a state of panic, but Afton, this is real for me. I am falling for you. I want to let this happen. I want to know what it feels like to be completely and madly in love with you." He knew that he already was.

Afton took in his words like the air she was breathing. And she allowed herself to feel his honesty and desperation for more of what she could give him, and for what they could share together. "I'm not reeling," she spoke, grinning. "I am on the verge of all of those feelings too. I'm just more hesitant than you are." She had complications and obligations, all of which she was not going to allow herself to focus on right now.

"Take your time," he reminded her. Just knowing she felt the same way had strengthened the hope in his heart — that he had for them.

"Help me take this risk," she began, and Knox stopped her.

"Don't look at it — at us and what we could share— as a hazard, or a gamble. Think of this as a chance, as the possibility and likelihood of something great happening. And lasting for the rest of forever."

She nodded along with his words. His beautiful words that had, like the lyrics of a song, drew her in and reached the depths of her. "How can I turn away from a chance like that?" she asked him.

He looked into her eyes, and she met him halfway. Their kiss felt different. It was slower, and just as eager, but this time they both trusted how it was safe to savor what was happening between them. And it was okay to believe that something special was just beginning. So much of the uncertainty was gone.

He took her by the hand and led her upstairs. More than anything, he wanted to be with her in his bed where they shared their first time. They would have a lifetime ahead of sex on the floor or the couch or the countertop. Knox was confident of that.

Her black shift dress with cap sleeves and a modest neckline fell to the floor. She was still wearing her high heels and bra and panties. Knox was shirtless in dress pants and bare feet. She felt sexy in those heels and left them on for awhile, before they reached the bed together again and had gradually gotten completely naked. He touched her so slowly she believed she would lose her mind. She ran her fingers through his wavy hair while he knew all the right places on her body to be attentive to. She tightened between her legs when his tongue found her nipples. She opened for him when he brushed his fingers across her folds. They kissed hard and deep and longingly. She opened her palms and smoothed them on his chest and down lower. She found herself wanting to put her mouth on him. So she gave in to that desire. The desire to make him feel the things she felt because of his attention to her needs. He pressed his hands down on her head. *God yes…* she heard him whisper. He was close, so close, and he wanted to stop her. She felt him pull away. "Let me love you," he said, and she felt tears spring to her eyes. Heartfelt, happy tears.

He laid her on her back and gave her the attention she lacked for too many years. And when she called out his name, it never sounded sweeter to him.

She watched him reach for the wrapper on the nightstand again, and he rolled the protection over himself. And then guided himself inside her. Their chests were together, skin on skin, their lips and tongues tasted each other, over and over. It was slow and steady and seductive and intoxicatingly powerful to be with him this way. He was deep inside of her, right where she wanted to keep him and continue to feel him. She felt a wave of release overcome her, almost in surprise, as he too freed himself. And they both recognized what was true of their connection just now. They had made love.

Chapter 16

Falling asleep in Knox's arms was a beautiful thing for her, until Afton woke up with a start, hours later, and realized it was morning. Knox was just as alarmed as she was to comprehend that it was 4 a.m.

She rushed out of bed, and back into her underwear and dress. "Oh God," she heard herself say, but refrained from speaking the rest, which primarily was *how in the world would she explain where she's been to Sam?*

"I'm really sorry I fell asleep, too," Knox spoke, quickly getting into his pants that had been wadded up on the floor all night long.

"It's on me," she told him. "I will work it out. I just have to go now!"

"Be safe," he told her, and hurried to kiss her lightly on the lips. He didn't follow her out the front door. He just hoped she would make it home without an explosive incident with her husband. He wasn't so sure that Afton was ready to be completely open with him, yet.

Afton carried her heels in her hand as she stepped off the front porch. It was still dark outside, but the street lights illuminated her path to the driveway to get into her car. She backed out cautiously, but quickly, and sped off down the road.

She never saw the young woman running through the cul de sac. The early-morning runner had already passed Knox's house once, but she had to go by it again as he lived at the end of a circle-drive with no outlet. It was her morning route for a safe run. She didn't live on Holly Avenue or in the historic part of Saint Paul at all, but she was training for a marathon and looked for well-protected areas of the city, including safe neighborhoods, to run long distances. Amy Drury saw her mother's car. There was no doubt it was her Highlander as the personalized license plates were Photo1. She slowed her pace when she saw her mother coming from a strange house, still wearing her dress from the day before. She stayed back, consumed with bewilderment, as she watched her drive away. *Was her mother seriously having an affair?*

Afton realized her cell phone was in her glove compartment. She attempted to reach for it while she was driving, barefoot nonetheless, but it ended up on the floor below the passenger seat. She left it because she was in too much of a hurry to get home. But she imagined the messages that were awaiting her. Sam was likely worried that something bad had happened to her because the last thing she said to him was she *would find a ride home.* And then her car was later gone from the garage. He probably had contacted her sisters, looking for her. The police could have been called. Great... a missing person's report was filed while she was asleep and naked in the arms of another man. Her armpits pooled with sweat in yesterday's dress. Her face was stained with day-old makeup. And she smelled of sex. That was her last crazy thought as she rolled her car over the curb that led up to her driveway. She pulled into the garage. Sam's car was in there. She kept her shoes off so she could remain as quiet as possible. Just in case, by some miracle, Sam had slept through her *disappearance*.

The house was dark and quiet. And Afton actually stopped holding her breath. There wasn't an entourage surrounding a distraught Sam in the living room. No one was worried about her all night long, because no one had known she was gone. She hoped for that more than anything as she went upstairs. But she did prepare herself to find him awake.

Their bedroom was dark, and the lump covered with the duvet on the far side of the bed was actually softly snoring. *Did Sam snore?* Afton was the soundest sleeper on the planet, practically comatose once her head hit the pillow as she had proven last night, so she really had no idea if he was plagued with noisy breathing while he slept beside her.

Afton quickly made her way into the master bathroom. She was going to shower extra early this morning, hoping if Sam awoke, he would only assume she had slept there last night and was already up and getting ready. That seemed too easy to pull off, so Afton didn't trust escaping trouble just yet.

Sneaking around had stressed her out. Afton's hands were trembling a little as she held her coffee cup in the kitchen. She remembered leaving her phone in the car, so she stepped out into the garage in her bare feet and white terrycloth robe. She opened the passenger door and found her phone still on the floor.

There were no messages from Sam. Not a single, *where are you?* Or, *when are you coming home?* She assumed she should have felt relief, all things considered. But she still felt like shaking her head because he had not even missed her. *She had been completely unreachable all night long.* Afton now carried very little guilt for cheating on Sam. Their marriage was over, and clearly had been for a very long time.

There were three other messages on her phone.

One hour ago, Knox texted, *Call me when you can.* Afton would call him, once Sam left for work. There was no fallout to report, like they both had expected the moment they woke up in each other arms and realized it was morning. Afton imagined having to answer to Sam, and telling him the truth. But she would not confess her sins without a confrontation about his relationship with Jess Robertson. Knox was concerned about Afton having to handle getting caught and the backlash that would follow, but a part of him already wanted their relationship to be out in the open. No more secrets or lies. He wanted to wine and dine her at the finest restaurants in the Twin Cities, and simply take a walk with her in the park.

A text from Jess, last night, caught Afton by surprise. *Can we talk sometime? Just the two of us.* Afton instantly speculated. *Would Jess confess? Did she truly think that Afton would just hand over her husband?* Afton needed to rethink that last thought. Sam wasn't hers to keep anymore, and their marriage had been dead for a very long time. Afton, again, felt apprehensive about the changes ahead in all of their lives.

Afton was startled when she noticed a missed call from Amy, thirty-five minutes ago. With no voicemail. A phone call from her daughter before 5 a.m. was unusual. She stepped back into the kitchen, and immediately tried to reach her. Her call went to voicemail. "Amy, what's going on? Call me back when you can."

Amy initially had called her mother, and then decided she wasn't ready to confront her. Instead, she sought advice, and comfort, from the aunt she always felt most connected to. Before the school day started for Laney, her niece had called her at an alarmingly early hour, in tears.

Laney set a glass of water down on the coffee table in front of her sofa. Amy was sitting on the floor near the furniture. She apologized for being *a sweaty mess* after her run. Laney shrugged that off, knowing whatever brought her niece there had been dire.

"Drink a little and take a few deep breaths. You're worrying me, you know," Laney sat down beside her on the floor. Her bed-hair was pulled up in a messy ponytail and she wore glasses, prior to putting in her contacts this morning. She crisscrossed her legs in her pink pajama pants and matching tank top. She had been in such a rush to let Amy in the front door, after she called her from right outside, that she forgot she wasn't wearing a bra. That was an after-thought now, but Laney let it go. Skye would have embraced it. Afton wouldn't think of doing something like that. Laney was definitely the middle sister. She did it, but thought twice about it.

"I know, I'm sorry," Amy spoke, massaging the muscles in her quads that were cramping from her long-distance run. A run that she pushed herself harder on, once she left Holly Avenue. Amy was small, barely five-foot-three, and one hundred and fifteen pounds. To Laney, she seemed even tinier right now. Her first thought was something terrible had happened to her in the dark, as she ran alone in the early morning hours. It wasn't the smartest, or safest, thing to do.

"Amy... did someone hurt you?" Laney came right out and asked what she was dreading. And she also would not hesitate to call the police if she had to.

"No, nothing like that. I'm fine. I'm just shaky and sick to my stomach because of what I saw."

"Just tell me. I can't help you if I don't know what it is."

"I saw mom's car in a neighborhood where I run. It's the historic part of town. I read the license plate as I passed by this house and I have no idea who lives there. I knew it was for sure mom's Highlander. When I circled back around, I saw her."

"You saw Afton this morning?"

"I run at 4 a.m., Aunt Laney."

Laney could not imagine why Afton was at someone else's house before sunrise. She immediately rehashed what part of town the Robertsons had lived in, assuming Afton could have been with Jess. "What was she doing?"

"Leaving. She was wearing the same black dress that she wore yesterday to Mark's funeral. I saw her rushing to her car, barefoot, and carrying her heels. It was dark, but there were street lights. It was so out of character for her, but it was my mom."

The part about wearing yesterday's clothes clearly sounded like a walk of shame, Laney fretted. But this was Afton they were talking about. Her older sister who could not have been a more of a straighter arrow in terms of making good choices and forever doing the right thing. To a fault. To a boring fault. Laney watched her niece break down.

"I – I can't get that image of her out of my head. I mean, come on, you know what it looked like. But, the thought of mom cheating? I can't comprehend that."

"We need to talk to her." Laney wanted answers, too. She also could not wait to call Skye, who would be just as flabbergasted and confused as she was about this possibility. This wasn't an ample opportunity for gossip. It was pure disbelief that needed to be shared among sisters — before they got to the truth.

"I called her, but she didn't answer," Amy admitted. "I don't even know what I was going to say over the phone. I just reacted and dialed her number."

"What time does your dad leave for work?" The very last thing Laney wanted was for Sam to be suspicious or overhear something.

"Around 6:30."

It was nearing that time now. Laney's husband and boys would be awake soon, and everyone had to get out the door for work and school.

"We can't rush this. How about I call your mom and see if she's free after work today? You and I could stop by. I won't tell her you're coming with me, but you can if you want to." Laney imagined Skye would as well, once she was aware. It would be like an intervention. Still, Laney could not envision Afton's life being in that sort of a mess.

Amy nodded. "I feel like such a baby about this. I mean, I am a grown adult. But it still hurts to think that my mom isn't who I believed she was."

"Hey, I know, I understand what you're saying. But, listen, we all make mistakes. We make choices for various reasons. Let's not judge your mom until we hear from her what's going on." A part of Laney believed that Afton really would have a reasonable explanation, and that there was no need to overreact.

Chapter 17

Laney's twelve-year-old twin boys attended seventh grade at the same middle school in Saint Paul where she taught eighth grade science for the past sixteen years. Because they were in the car with her, Laney hadn't been able to make the phone call that was weighing on her mind. She wanted to reach out to Skye first.

When she entered her empty classroom, which was also a science lab, she flipped on the lights and pressed her phone to her ear. Skye answered on the second ring. "Hey Laney... Isn't it a school day?"

"The bell rings in twenty minutes," she stated, putting down her tote bag, that she brought home every evening, on the chair behind her desk. "But, this can't wait." Skye paused to hear more. "Amy was out for a ridiculously early run this morning, and she saw Afton leaving a strange house on the historic side of town, on Holly Avenue."

Skye's eyes widened on the opposite end of the phone. There was only one explanation. Afton was still seeing her new lover. A one-time hook-up must have turned into an affair.

"Did Amy confront her?"

"What? No. She came to me, upset and confused. Aren't you at all surprised by this? We're talking about Afton here — the same person who claims to hate sex."

"Yeah I know," Skye was careful to answer.

"Are you already aware of something? Afton confided in you, didn't she?" Laney suddenly felt like the odd sister out. The truth was, she didn't think any of them were close, but knowing Skye and Afton might be had stung a little more than she expected.

"Only because I caught her in a lie with Sam. She fabricated a story about babysitting Bella into the wee hours. I called her out."

"She lied? Are we even talking about the same person?" Laney glanced at the round clock on the wall above the doorway. She was going to need more time for this conversation.

"I know. We only talked about it once. I was hoping it just happened that one time. Afton hasn't told me anything more since, even after I've reached out to her."

Laney sighed. "I actually feel sorry for Sam."

"Well don't. He's an asshole. I blame him for Afton turning to someone else so quickly after she found out that he's screwing around."

"Oh God... does Afton know with who?"

"You have to promise me to keep your cool. It's someone you know. And you're at school, so you cannot react by telling the first colleague you see in the hallway." Skye imagined that rumor circulating through the entire school while Jess was on personal leave following the loss of her husband.

"Jesus, Skye. You have my word. Who is it?"

"Jess Robertson."

"They are close friends! All four of them were," Laney added, thinking of Mark. Everyone at the funeral service truly seemed to be in mourning. And perhaps they were. But Laney questioned how Afton could play the part of a good friend, knowing what she knew about Jess.

"Exactly. Afton was hurt when she found out, but she never confronted anyone. Not Sam or Jess. I honestly think she's reeling, which explains the bad girl that has emerged." Skye suppressed a giggle, and Laney heard her.

"Unbelievable. So, she does like sex after all?"

"She does now." They both laughed.

"Listen, I need to go," Laney stated. "We have to talk to her. Will you go with me? Maybe after school today?" Laney considered including Amy, but she didn't get off work at the dental office until after five p.m. And, honestly, Laney wanted to give her sister a chance to explain herself without her child present, even if she was an adult. Afton deserved that advanced warning to avoid further humiliation.

"Yes. Will you call her, or should I?" Skye was willing.

"I'll text her. Hopefully we can stop by her studio," Laney suggested, thinking they could have some privacy there.

"Sounds good. And Laney?"

"Yeah?" she watched two of her students walk in, both were preteen girls acting as if they were much older.

"I'm glad you reached out. We both need to be there for Afton."

Laney caught herself smiling into the phone. "Me too. See you later today."

Afton heard Sam coming down the stairs. On cue, it was thirty minutes before seven o'clock, and he was dressed and ready for work. When he reached the kitchen, she forced herself to make eye contact with him. *Oh the guilt though. She was one of those women. But damn it. He was also one of those men.*

"*Morning,*" she said first.

"How late were you out?" he questioned her.

"Too late, and I'm feeling it this morning. I fell asleep on Skye's sofa." Fabricating another easily-believable babysitting story came to mind first.

"Skye needs to get a regular sitter and stop taking advantage of you." Afton only nodded. *Let's not bash her innocent sister.*

A matter of minutes later, Sam had full a cup of coffee, an almost-burnt piece of toast, and he was walking out the door. Everyone puttered through predictable routines in life, but this daily one of Sam's was beginning to annoy her. In any case, Afton was relieved to see him leave. Turns out, her recklessness last night was a nonissue.

She went upstairs to blow dry her hair, but before she did, she received a text. Her first thought was Amy. But it was Laney.

Could I stop by the studio after school today? It's important.

Reaching out like that was out of the ordinary for Laney. Afton immediately assumed Skye couldn't keep a secret, but she didn't want to jump to that conclusion. So, she replied, *Sure. I will be there.*

After three o'clock, both Laney and Skye came through the door of the studio. Afton looked up from her on-screen photo edits. "Both of you? Why do I suddenly feel like I'm being ganged up on?" Afton zeroed in on Skye. She gave her a look of disapproval, as if to convey, *you never could keep a secret to save your life.*

"Don't blame Skye," Laney immediately spoke up, and she was quick because Skye was always the first to defend herself in any situation. "I called her with my own suspicions."

Afton didn't want to say a word to either of them until she knew exactly why they had shown up as if they were on some sort of a mission to ambush her. "Will one of you please tell me what is going on?"

"Amy runs very early in the morning," Laney began, and Afton instantly feared something happened. She had, though, received a brief text in response to her voicemail this morning and she knew her daughter was at work. "Today, she was running in the historic part of town, on Holly Avenue." Afton felt the color drain from her face as Laney continued to speak. "She saw you, Aft."

Afton covered her mouth. Shame shot through her. "What did she see exactly?"

"Your car on the driveway. You, as you were leaving a strange house — apparently looking disheveled."

"Are you still seeing the same guy?"

How both of her sisters sought answers forced Afton to face a new reality that she hadn't yet. *People knew what she was doing.* "I have to try to explain this to Amy," Afton began, "but how? How do I tell her that I've been with another man, when I'm still married to her father?"

"Sam hasn't exactly been a saint either," Skye stated firmly. Afton then at least felt like someone was on her side.

"As Skye has said, he's an asshole. But, come on Afton, did you have to go and do the same thing?" Laney was certainly the most judgmental of the three of them, especially when it came to relationships. *Likely, because her marriage to Brad was perfect.*

"It wasn't like that," Afton defended herself. She still, however, questioned if she would have been as willing to free herself to be with Knox, if she had not known about Sam and Jess.

"Let's not go there," Skye stopped the two of them. "We are here because we want to know what's going on. And then there's Amy."

Afton wasn't at all confident that she could explain her own thoughts and actions to her daughter when she was still in the beginning stages of this whirlwind. "I stayed overnight with him. We didn't mean to, but we fell asleep. I was emotionally spent from Mark's funeral. Sam wanted to go to the office late in the day, but I suspected he ran back to Jess. I needed some comfort. And I suddenly have someone in my life who wants to offer that to me, and he does."

"It's sex," Skye interjected. "How can you already be sure that he wants anything more than that?"

"I ask myself that when I'm not with him, but when we are together and talking and connecting in so many ways, I don't doubt this is a relationship that we could build on."

"You're going to end up hurt," Laney tried to be logical.

"Maybe," Afton all but shrugged her shoulders.

"We just want you to be careful," Skye stated. "You basically know nothing about this guy."

Afton shook her head at her little sister. "Don't be a hypocrite."

"Okay. I deserved that," Skye agreed, "but let me tell you something. What you're doing... it's a lonely way to live." Skye had never admitted that to anyone before. She was afraid of commitment, so she ran from any man who was relationship potential. After she slept with him.

"I think you both know that my marriage has been a really lonely place, too, for a very long time," Afton had their attention. "I haven't admitted that to myself, until now. I don't think Sam

121

would disagree with me. I'm fifty years old. At least half of my life is behind me. If I don't live the rest of it now, really live it, I'm going to lose that chance. I don't know if I want to spend those years in shared silence with Sam. It's unhealthy for both of us to just exist in a marriage." As Afton said those things to her sisters, she realized she needed to be saying all of that to Sam.

Chapter 18

On her way home, Afton called Knox. She prepared herself to leave a message as he was likely still at the hospital. Instead, she immediately heard his voice on the other end.

"I've been worried about you," was how he answered her call. "How did things go at home?"

She was already touched by his concern. "I really wasn't missed," she told him, "so I breathed a sigh of relief and let it go."

"Good for you," he smiled into the phone.

"But after talking to my sisters, I realized that I can't keep doing this." Knox froze, thinking that she was prepared to end what had just gotten started between them. "I want to talk to Sam. I need to be honest, and I am going to expect the same from him in return. I can't keep lying and sneaking around. That's not who I am, or how I want to live my life. Knox, I'm going to end my marriage."

He sat in his office, with both of his elbows resting on his desktop. His white lab coat was draped over the chair behind him. The sleeves of his powder-blue button down shirt were rolled up to his elbows. His brownish-blond hair was tousled but it was a typical organized messy look that he had grown out since his divorce. His face beamed with happiness, listening to Afton's words. She wanted closure, and a new beginning. This was yet another step that would lead the two of them closer together. He was certain of that.

"I don't wish you that kind of pain, because I've been there and it hurts to end a marriage, but Afton — you know what this means for us."

"I know," it was her turn to smile into the phone. Having him in her life, in her corner, gave her such courage.

Afton was turning off the lights in her studio, and prepared to close for the day. She had three senior photo sessions scheduled for the next three days. Business was steady, and she still loved photography after all these years. It was the one constant in her life. The creativity that she put into it, fed her soul. She thought of her grandmother and the life lesson on personal fulfillment. *Find something to refuel yourself. You must do that for yourself. Don't live solely for the sake of others. A woman needs more than that, just the same as a man does.*

Being with Knox had also refueled her. As a woman. And, as a human being looking for more out of life than what she had. Afton actually believed that Sam would understand. He, too, deserved more. More than what she could give him.

Afton didn't cook dinner too often anymore. It was pointless, because she and Sam rarely shared a meal. After their children moved out and started lives of their own, Afton got into the habit of preparing a few meals ahead. Right now, she thought about reheating something leftover. But she felt too nervous to eat. She sipped a glass of wine at the island, as sort of a confidence lift, or a courage boost. She was seriously going to do this.

When the sound of the garage door caught her attention, Afton waited for Sam in the kitchen.

"Hello," he said, almost reacting as if he was surprised to see her. *She had been gone a lot lately.*

"Hi. Would you like a drink with me?"

Sam dropped his keys on the table. "You're not eating tonight?"

"Maybe later," she stated.

Sam walked over to the refrigerator, opened the door, looked in, and then closed it again. "I'll pass on the drink. Jess asked me to stop by tonight. She's overwhelmed with some of the paperwork that's come in. Mark handled things like she's having to cipher through. Bills mainly, I guess. I agreed to help," he paused. "Did you want to come along?"

Afton thought of Jess' text to her that she had both partially forgotten and halfheartedly ignored. "I don't think so. Three's a crowd sometimes."

Sam stared at her. His glasses sat low on his nose, and he looked at her overtop. That gesture was one of an old man, but he wasn't there yet. It dawned on her now that this was the extent of their growing old together after twenty-five years. "What does that mean?" he asked.

"We need to talk, Sam. Before you run to Jess Robertson again." At this rate, Afton was beginning to make this conversation about Sam's affair. Not hers. That wasn't entirely fair, she knew, but it had to be said nonetheless.

He walked over to the refrigerator and grabbed a beer anyway. She watched him twist the cap, and tip the glass bottle to his mouth. A generous swig later, he looked at her. "Mark was our friend. The least we can do is be there for Jess and the kids if they need anything."

"Like a ride home?" Afton asked, feeling the hurt and anger surface from the night she followed the two of them and discovered they were having an affair.

"Do you have something that you want to say to me?" Sam put her on the spot.

"I know, Sam. I know about the two of you." She had no idea the length of their affair, and quite honestly, she didn't really want to know.

Sam stared long and hard at his wife before he spoke. There wasn't surprise in his eyes. It was more like he was studying her, and intently trying to figure out what was sifting through her mind. *Was she angry? Hurt? Would she cry, beg, or make demands?*

"Jess Robertson isn't my wife. She's a friend with benefits. She fulfills a need, my sexual need. That's all we are to each other."

Afton scoffed. "So you're friends and lovers? How convenient for you both. Poor Mark. He was a good man and did not deserve that from his wife."

"You didn't include yourself in that pity party," Sam stated, clearly being snarky. "Could that be because you, in the back of your mind, knew I had to be getting it somewhere. Of course you knew. A man can't go without forever."

"I failed at trusting my friend," Afton stated, "but I never put too much thought into trusting you." She watched her husband crease his brow. "No. There isn't much of anything left between us. We share a house, car payments, utility bills, children who rarely come around. Oh, and a bed, but not really…"

"That was your prerogative." He threw sex in her face.

She nodded. "It was. I didn't want it. And, with you, I never liked it." Afton had his attention now. "I have discovered, though, sex is pleasurable and something that I am able to desire and enjoy."

"So an eye for an eye? That's how this is now for you?" Sam had a difficult time concealing his surprise. *His wife had cheated on him.*

"I don't see it that way, but okay," she stated. "So where do we stand now that I know you haven't kept your dick in your pants around Jess, and I've also admitted to being in someone else's bed? I think we both know a few good divorce attorneys in the Twin Cities to help us go our separate ways."

"Nothing needs to change," Sam spoke, calmly, as if he was truly unaffected by all of this. "We will still co-exist. It's what we do. You need me, just as I rely on you. Someday we will share grandchildren, and later great-grandchildren. Our family will continue to grow and flourish. You know that I come from generation after generation of well-respected people who didn't believe in divorce. I intend to carry out that tradition."

"The tradition of a successful marriage?" she asked him. "Clearly, we have failed at that. I want a divorce, Sam."

"You appear to be on a high right now. Possibly it's this new leaf you have turned over. Or perhaps you're finding yourself caught up in a whirlwind that's also clarified as a mid-life crisis. Go, have your orgasms and explore those sexual positions and fantasies that used to appall you — or at least make you blush. But you know where your home is afterward."

"You're not hearing me." This was the last thing that Afton expected from him. She imagined he would practically skip out of the kitchen, eager to indulge in being a free man.

"Oh but I am," he chuckled a little under his breath, and it unnerved her. "Until death do us part, Afton. You heard me."

"You think that I am inferior to you? I'm done, Sam. *We* have been finished for a very long time."

"Run around as often as you like," he told her. "Just don't flaunt it publicly. Don't embarrass yourself. But do return to this house, and to our forever-binding marriage."

"You've lost your mind!" she reacted.

"Ah the mind is my most favorite thing, you know that," he told her. "Let this sink in to yours. I will simplify my point for you. If you leave me, I'll bury you."

Afton wasn't fazed by his threat. "I have a withstanding reputation in this town. I own a business, strictly in my name." As if he needed to be reminded that her earnings were deposited in her own separate bank account, still listed under Afton Gallant, her maiden name. She began Afton Photography prior to Sam. And he never objected to her independence. "I have the love and respect of my children and my family. How is it that you think you can take anything away from me?"

"I suppose the term bury can be interpreted more than one way. What I meant was, bury — as in Mark Robertson."

Chapter 19

Sam made his threat and left. He thought his point was clear, and that there would be nothing to think twice about. Because nothing would change. Afton, however, wanted to make changes in her life now more than ever. This wasn't about running into the arms of another man. This was about her freedom and her dignity. She was not a woman controlled by a man. She never had been. Sam knew that all too well, as he had turned to at least one other woman to heed the desires that his wife would not.

Afton called Knox. He didn't expect what she told him, and his first instinct was to protect her. "Pack your things and come stay with me, at least until we know you're safe." He veered off from scaring her away with any immediate commitment, and hoped she would hear that in his offer.

"I can't do that. I am not afraid of my husband. He throws words around. He's a psychiatrist, and I suppose an overconfident one at that. If I leave my home, I want it to be on my terms, a credit to my independence. I'd like to have a place to call my own." Afton would miss everything about the home she had for half of her life. There were markings and lived-in parts of that two-story Victorian house that reminded her of the precious memories with her children. And with Sam, too. They shared happier times that were behind them now. And Afton was ready to let it all go.

"Just for tonight then?" Knox pressed her. But the way that he tried to be cautiously insistent was a welcomed change than what she had just experienced with Sam. It was Sam's way or no way. With Knox, he told her what he wanted, and then allowed her to make up her own mind. That may have had everything to do with making the comparison of a well-worn relationship versus a brand new one, but Afton still noticed the vast difference in those two men.

"I can agree to that," she stated, but she would return home in the morning.

Afton did pack an overnight bag, but felt strange doing it. She wanted to be with Knox. She was ready to leave behind her life as she knew it. Even still, the newness of everything was going to take some getting used to.

As she backed her car out of the garage and down the driveway, her phone rang. It was Jess. She likely had spoken to Sam and was calling to what? *Beg and plead for forgiveness? To tell Afton that she wanted Sam all to herself?* Those were random thoughts, but what she really wanted to know was, *Did their friendship ever mean anything to Jess?* She ignored the call.

And then Jess immediately called back.

Afton picked up the phone and answered it. She could have turned it off, but she didn't. And she had no idea why she was giving Jess this chance to speak.

"I can't imagine why you would be calling me now," Afton spoke the moment she accepted the call.

"Afton, please just hear me out. There's trouble. I can't talk about this over the phone. Will you meet me somewhere? Not your house or mine. Sam just left my house and I only was able to buy so much time."

Trouble? Buy time? Afton wasn't following this at all. "Jess I think we should just leave this alone. Friendships end all the time. You obviously were not who I believed."

"I know, I know!" Jess sounded desperate. "Five minutes, that's all. And then if you still want to tell me to go to hell, I will give up."

Afton sighed. There was desperation in her voice. "I am leaving my driveway now. If you want privacy, meet me at the studio."

"Yes. Thank you!"

Afton ended their call.

Afton arrived first. She parallel parked along the street that lined a portion of the business district in downtown Saint Paul. There was nothing for her to carry in. She didn't have her camera bag in tow because this was not about work. *But what was this?* Jess had not made a lot of sense on the phone. And Afton actually felt uncomfortable about seeing her.

She unlocked the door, flipped on the lights, and waited. It was merely a matter of seconds until Jess came through the door. Afton then locked it behind her.

"I'm closed," she spoke to clarify why she locked the door, after she brushed past her. Their shoulders almost touched.

"Afton…" Jess slowly turned her body toward her. Afton was in such close proximity to the door that she could have pressed her back against it. But she stayed very still, and forced herself to look at her *friend*. She was a beauty. Just stunning. Her long dark hair was down well past her shoulders. She wore eyeliner and mascara, and a soft brown shade of lipstick. The rest of her face was makeup-free. Her eyes were sad, Afton noticed again. She had the same forlorn look since her husband passed away. Afton didn't believe a person could fake their grief. Not like that. Still, she was so confused by Jess and Sam. Sam was an asshole, as Skye liked to say, but Jess was not that kind of a woman. At least Afton had never perceived her as a heartless whore. "I know what you must think of me. And I deserve your wrath."

"I didn't agree to meet with you to yell and scream and fight. I am past the bullshit in my life. I told Sam that I want a divorce, and he's not hearing me. But, he will, because we are done. So, take him. You can gladly have him. I certainly don't want him anymore."

"He's blackmailing me."

Afton stepped away from the door and closer to Jess. "What?"

"We've been lovers since the kids were in middle school," Jess admitted, and Afton rolled her eyes. *How could she have been so oblivious?* "Neither of us ever wanted more than what we were doing. And then Mark died."

"I don't understand," Afton interrupted. "Sam doesn't believe in divorce, but if he divorced me, he could have you, as Mark is no longer in the way." She meant no disrespect to Mark, but her words made sense if two unavailable people were screwing around for years.

"You said it. He doesn't believe in divorce. I don't want to be married to him anyway. I never have! Afton, I'm really afraid of him."

Afton creased her brow. She could still see the two of them together in the parking lot that night. Walking in sync. Touching. Laughing. There was no fear. Jess Robertson was a liar. "Why?"

"Mark was seeing Sam, professionally." This was something that Afton had not been aware of. "You know that

134

Mark had a heart murmur that was first detected in his teenage years. He took medication and saw a cardiologist annually. Sam convinced him, months ago, that innovative, holistic therapy could gradually ween him off the medication for his heart. Mark's weight was a lifelong struggle for him, and excessive weight gain was a side effect from his meds. He was convinced that Sam was right, because he started to feel better after the therapy sessions. He decreased his medicine and slowly began to lose weight."

"Are you telling me that Sam used his medical knowledge to convince Mark to stop treating his heart murmur? That's absurd. Jesus. Is that... no... that's what caused the heart attack!"

"Sam didn't want me to have an autopsy done. He told me that we all knew Mark had a fragile heart. I had one done anyway. It was conclusive. If Mark had not stopped taking his meds for his mitral valve regurgitation, he would still be alive." Jess looked as if she was going to either be sick, or burst into tears. Afton just stood there, silenced and shocked. But she believed her. Afton then asked the only question echoing in her mind.

"How is Sam blackmailing you?" Afton concluded that he must have known Jess blamed him for Mark's death, and he retaliated as only Sam would. With a power play.

"When I confronted him, he denied any wrongdoing. I lost it. I called him a murderer. And that's when he threatened me. He said he will make sure that my reputation is discredited, as everyone will know that I am an adulteress. I will lose my job. And, now, he came up with some sort of binding agreement for me to sign, promising that I never reveal what I know. And, the most absurd part… he is forbidding me to move on with my life. Now, or in the future. I can never date or remarry. Sam owns me, he claims." Afton didn't react. But she believed this was as ridiculous as Sam threating to *bury* her. Afton realized then that Sam had actually insinuated his part in Mark's death. "That's why I am afraid of him now. He expects me to sign that agreement."

"How is something like that even legally binding? Is Sam's attorney some sort of wack job?"

"He claimed it was legit. I don't know. I am reeling. I lost Mark. I don't even know how to stand on my own two feet without him."

Afton stared at Jess before she spoke. "If he meant that much to you… why Jess? Why did you betray him for most of your marriage?"

Jess sighed and Afton watched the tears pool in her eyes. "Mark took so much medication." She didn't need to list his ailments. Afton knew he had high blood pressure, diabetes, and his heart issue, just to think of a few. "He had zero sex drive. His weight played a huge factor in that, too, I know, and I couldn't change that about him. About us. And then, Sam confessed to me that you and he never—"

"How convenient for the two of you," Afton interjected.

"I'm sorry, Afton. God, you will never know how much I hate what I've done."

The image surfaced in her mind again of the two of them in each other's arms. "Of course you are remorseful now that Mark paid for your sins with his life!"

"That's not fair," Jess started to cry.

"Life isn't fair, friend." Afton was being snarky, but she believed she had every right to be.

"I need your help. I couldn't tell anyone else," Jess practically pleaded with her.

"Sam has to be stopped," Afton agreed, "but I don't know how to trust you anymore. I hear about friendships that withstand it all. I felt like we were pretty close, but you hardly set the benchmark for what it's like to be a friend through and through. Did we ever truly connect on a genuine level?" Afton continued speaking her mind, "I care about you, Jess, but I can live without you."

"I purposely held back. I didn't want to get too close, and eventually end up hurting you like I have. I adore you, and all that you stand for. You will never be a woman like me." Jess had not believed Sam when he said Afton was unfaithful to him.

Afton was silent. But what Jess said resonated with her. She was a woman who made both selfless and selfish choices. She was no different or better than anyone else. She had no right to judge Jess, despite everything.

"He has to be stopped," Afton spoke. "What can we do together to make that happen?"

Jess smiled through her tears. And then Afton reached for her hand.

Chapter 20

Afton and Jess agreed that she should stay overnight with her daughter. Jess could use the excuse that she was drowning in her grief and did not want to be alone. That escape would keep Sam away, and no one would assume anything of it. Afton then arrived late at Knox's house.

He met her at the door, and took her hand. He missed her. "You're not bruised and bloody," he stated. "I assume there was no catfight?" Knox had known she met with Jess.

Afton giggled. "I'm not that kind of girl."

"Somehow I guessed that," Knox smiled.

"We talked, a lot," Afton began, as she had no intention of keeping secrets from Knox. She told him everything from Sam threatening her life, to Sam feeling challenged to ruin Jess' life. When she finally stopped with the revelations, Knox just sat there after he took it all in.

"You have to get away from him. Both of you do. He's not a stable man, and that puts the people around him in danger. I won't let him hurt you, Afton. I think we need to go to the police."

"On what grounds? A few threats? No one can prove Mark went off his medicine because Sam played mind games with him. He will not be charged, but reputations will be ruined for sure. I don't want that for myself, or for Jess."

"You are remarkable, and you don't even realize it," Knox told her, as they sat close on his sofa.

She shook her head. "I never said I forgave her."

"Doesn't matter. You still have a big heart."

"Nahh, it's my boobs that are big. Have you seen these girls?" She gestured to her chest, and giggled.

"Oh I've done more than look," Knox chuckled. "I'm glad you're staying with me tonight," he said, moving toward her lips. Their kiss lingered and then quickly intensified. And somewhere in the midst of their fiery passion, she said, "so am I."

The following morning, Afton was back home in the kitchen, in her robe and drinking coffee, when Sam came downstairs. He was ready for work, and she was prepared to have a conversation with him.

"Good morning," he said first.

"Is it?" Afton asked him, and he disregarded her words. Her cell phone was on audio record, face down on the island, close to her coffee mug. "I suppose it's a better morning than the one not too long ago when you came downstairs with the awful news about Mark."

"Right," he agreed.

"Now that we've all had some time to think about it, we knew he had a preexisting heart condition that he was being treated for, for years. I mean, were you completely surprised by his death?"

"Yeah I was. Mark was the kind of guy we all expected to live forever, even though he was unhealthy in many ways." Sam had his coffee poured and he was toasting that one piece of white bread.

"Was there an autopsy done?"

"I don't think so. In my opinion, there was no need to search for a cause."

"Really? I think it would bring closure. I mean, I would want to know."

Sam took the piece of dry toast and held it between his teeth while he carried the coffee mug in one hand. And with his free hand, he picked up Afton's phone, turned it over, and stopped the audio record. "We never talk this much in the morning," he said, once he took the toasted bread out of his mouth. "Nice try, Afton."

She started to breathe again after he closed the door behind him. Jess was right — he was guilty. And Afton now believed Knox's assumption was accurate too — the people around Sam were in danger. But Sam was a man who was always one step ahead of everyone else.

Afton again called Knox and told him everything. His first response was for her to permanently get out of that house. She agreed she would, and soon, but she had a senior photo session today. She would call him later.

Afton also compiled a lengthy text and sent it to both of her sisters. She told Laney and Skye about her revealing conversation with Jess, and how she believed her accusations toward Sam. He was guilty. She also informed them of her failed attempt to record him this morning, and his reaction to that. Afton concluded the text, sounding like their big sister would — *Don't worry about me, everything will work out.*

Afton tried to put all of this out of her mind. She had no other choice, as she was working. She spent the entire morning shooting on location with a seventeen-year-old young man and his mother. A majority of the photographs were taken at Como Lake, as fishing was the boy's thing. At one point, Afton suggested they omit the props —the canoe, and the fishing gear— and only capture him and the water. Afton imagined the water as merely the backdrop. But there was a damaged tree offshore that had split and a portion of it was leaning far over the water. Afton was eyeing a way to frame the shot, with that imperfect tree, when the young man —dressed simply in faded jeans, a red t-shirt, and brown boat shoes— climbed onto the parts of the tree that led him over the water. There was a farther, lone branch that he eagerly and confidently attempted to make his way onto. His mother balked at the idea. Afton also warned him that it could snap under his weight. His response took Afton by sheer surprise. He had been quiet, and a little challenging to warm up. His smiled looked more forced than natural for most of the photos that Afton had viewed on the display screen on the back of her Canon as she worked. But when she watched him take a chance out on that limb, and she heard his reasoning, the vibe of that session instantly changed.

"I'm going to trust that it will hold me. I don't know for sure that it will, but who cares? If I fall, I'll swim."

If I fall, I'll swim.

Those simple words resonated with her. Afton's life mirrored that questionable branch hanging above the lake water. She had not necessarily been looking to change her life — or to spread her wings somewhere new and different and unknown. It just happened to her. And now, she was ready to trust that if she fell, she would have the confidence and the strength to carry on.

Chapter 21

Her natural curly hair was frizzy from sweating in the heat and humidity. Her skin felt itchy from the grass and some of the tall weeds she had trekked through near the lake. All Afton wanted to do was strip out of her clothes and take a hot shower. She was driving home to do just that when her cell phone buzzed on the passenger seat beside her. It was a text from Jess.

I am at home. Sam's car just pulled up. I'm scared of what he might do.

It was late afternoon. Afton had never known Sam to leave early from work. But as she had discovered lately, after twenty-five years of marriage, she hardly knew him at all. Afton didn't reply to the text. She just stopped her car and changed directions with absolutely no idea of what would happen now.

Sam's car was on the driveway when she got there. Afton parked her vehicle curbside on the street and made her way up the sidewalk that led to the front door. She could hear voices from inside, Sam's was raised. She rang the doorbell. A moment later, Jess pulled open the door. Afton could see the relief in her eyes.

Jess stepped back for Afton to come inside.

"Afton? What are you doing here?" Sam's blue tie was loosened around his neck. The sleeves of his white dress shirt were rolled back to his elbows. The sunlight pouring in from all the windows in the Robertson's living room made Sam's once dark hair look grayer.

"I stopped by to check on Jess," she answered him. "And you?"

"The same," he nodded, with a firm glance in Jess' direction, as if he expected her to comply. Afton noticed he rolled a stack of papers in his hands. "But given how you know our history, why would you care how Jess is doing?"

"Your history, as you put it, is disgusting to me," Afton began speaking and she didn't look at Jess. Only at her husband. "But there comes a time in life when you have to stand up for what's right. And the way you are treating Jess is wrong. I will not let you bully her or try to control her."

Sam chuckled. And Afton shared a look with Jess. She looked scared, and there was something about her fear that empowered Afton to be stronger. "As far as I see it, you aren't much freer than Jess. Face it. I'm here to stay, ladies."

"I no longer want to share my life with you, Sam. And Jess, well, she needs you to get out of her way while she grieves for Mark, and tries to begin again on her own."

"I have no intention of changing anything," Sam spoke confidently, and Afton was annoyed. She had reached the point where she was no longer hurt or angry or upset with him. She was simply done. And he wasn't hearing her. "Just go, Afton. Get the hell out of here. Go take some measly pictures of someone, and I will see you at home later."

"Do you even hear yourself?" Afton pressured him. "For a man who has spent his entire career helping others with your doctor of the mind degree, you sure are unrealistic when it comes to your own problems. Nothing gets accomplished with ultimatums and demands." Afton could see that she had gotten to him. Perspiration beaded on his brows, and he intentionally bit the inside of his cheek. That, she was well aware, was a nervous tendency of his.

"I told you that I will ruin your credibility, both of you!" he raised his voice.

"What do you think we care about more, Sam? Our reputations or our freedom?"

Jess' eyes widened. Afton Drury had a backbone like she never witnessed before. She was a good one to have on her side.

"I want to continue my conversation with Jess, alone," Sam stared at his wife.

"No." Afton was adamant.

"Get out!" Sam screamed at her, and Afton felt empowered. The always calm and collected man lost his cool. What she didn't expect was for Sam to lunge toward her. He grabbed her by the throat. His eyes that bore directly down into hers were not those of her husband. This was a man she didn't know anymore. He was no longer all-commanding with compliant people at his mercy. Afton stood in his way, and she fought him. And then he retaliated with violence. This time, fear shot through her.

She struggled with him. They knocked over a large ceramic vase that crashed and broke on the hardwood floor at their feet. Afton struggled to get both of his hands free from the fierce grip around her neck. She shut her eyes and momentarily willed herself the strength to fight him off. And in the few seconds when her world was temporarily black, Jess reacted. Sam and Afton were struggling near the fireplace. His intention was only to scare her into leaving, but he had taken his anger too far. Jess reacted out of pure panic and desperation when she reached for the fireplace poker, raised it high in the air behind Sam, and struck him over the head.

He instantly fell to the floor and onto a glass cherub figurine that was displayed below the mantle. It was gifted to her at Mark's funeral. And it was now shattered shards beneath Sam's limp body. Afton struggled to take in air. She bent to her knees, and coughed. Long and hard. On the floor, she stared down at Sam, and then back up at Jess. The poker was still clenched in both of her hands. And those hands were now trembling.

"Oh God, Oh God… no no no… is he?"

Afton moved slowly on her knees, toward her husband. Her lifeless husband. There was a squiggly line of blood trickling down the side of his face from the open wound on the top of his head. Afton checked for a pulse. There was none.

She immediately pulled back from him, and off the floor. Jess dropped the fireplace poker that clanged at her feet, and she too backed away. The two of them huddled against a far wall.

"He was going to kill me, right?" Afton asked the woman beside her, the woman who was in the very same room and witnessed Sam's uncontrollable rage.

Jess nodded her head repeatedly. Her mascara was running underneath both of her eyes. Her long dark hair, pulled back into a ponytail, was coming undone. "I had to do something."

"You saved my life," Afton spoke in barely a whisper.

"And now mine is over. Unless you count prison as life."

"Not if we have the same story. Sam was going to kill us both."

"What are you saying?" Jess asked her.

"Light the fireplace," Afton told her.

"Why?"

Afton rushed over to the place on the floor where those papers in Sam's hands had fallen. She picked them up. "What is this?" Afton glanced down.

"The agreement that Sam was forcing me to sign, for my silence, and to bind me to him."

"Light a fire. We are burning these."

"Afton, it's eighty-five degrees outside. If we light a fire and then call the police," she gestured to the floor at Sam's lifeless body, "that is going to scream suspicious."

Afton was quiet, as she started to think about all of the questions and repercussions that lied ahead — if they called the police.

They shared silence until Jess finally reacted first. "What are you thinking?" The only thing Jess could imagine right now was confessing everything to the police, the entire truth, and still having to pay for taking a man's life.

"Where did you and Sam get together all those times? Here?"

Jess looked dismayed. "What in the hell? Why are you bringing that up now?"

"Just answer me. Did you ever meet him anywhere but in this house?"

Jess paused. "About ten miles from here, there's a motel, it's called Norwood Inn. We were there... in the daytime."

"Let's go. I will follow you there. Drive my car, and I'll drive Sam's."

"I don't understand," Jess stated, stepping closer to Afton and grabbing her by the shoulders with both of her hands. "You're not making any sense right now."

"We need a place to leave his abandoned car. That seems logical to me, as he's been seen there before."

Jess didn't ask yet what that meant for Sam's body.

Chapter 22

Afton sat on one of the matching mahogany-brown leather sofas in her house. Sam insisted on that color, in leather, she remembered. She would have chosen something brighter, like the seafoam suede set that was also at the same furniture store that day.

On the other sofa, directly across from her, was Detective Curt Weh from the Saint Paul Police Department. "If you can think of anything else that would help us find your husband, no matter how trivial it may seem, please share it. We hope to find him soon and bring him back home."

Afton nodded her head. They had already discussed Sam's clients, and the possibility of any one of them who may have wanted to harm him. Afton had not been able to help much. Sam's practice had become something he kept separate from their lives. Afton shared all there was to share with the police, or so she had claimed. Her story was told. *Her husband never came home from work. That wasn't unusual, Afton told them, as she had tolerated the philandering for most of their marriage. She admitted how they lived separate lives, and she believed she was convincing as she appeared unaffected by that. She wasn't distraught, but she wanted her husband found.* The police quickly located Sam's car at a local motel. It was locked and there was nothing inside — no keys, wallet, or cell phone. The front desk clerk had no record of Sam checking in that day, but they knew of him. He had been there before. They couldn't say who he met there, as Sam Drury always checked in alone.

Her children joined her in the living room when Detective Weh left. They both sat down on same sofa. Afton walked over to them, and sat on edge of the coffee table in front of them, in very close proximity.

"I'm sorry, mom," her son, Latch, spoke first. She reached for his hand. She always thought he looked like her own father, his maternal grandfather, more than he resembled Sam. Both of her children had naturally brownish blond hair and hazel eyes.

"Why did you two stay together all these years?" her daughter asked, as she now was well aware that both of her parents were unfaithful to each other. Neither of Afton's children had known Jess was involved with Sam. And that truth would stay untold.

"Years go by faster than you realize," Afton began to explain. "We all go through the motions of everyday life, and routines. Your father was content as we were, and I guess I was guilty of that as well."

"They think he ran off with one of his lovers, don't they?" Latch asked his mother. He assumed the rumors were true, and his father had *gotten around*.

"I assume so."

"What if someone hurt him, or worse?" Amy stated, putting a palm to her mouth as she muffled a sob.

"Our minds will imagine the worst until we know something factual, but I believe that your father is gone and he's never coming back. He will either stay away because he wants to, or because—"

"He's dead," Latch finished her words for her.

"First Mark, and now dad. This is unreal," Amy spoke again in disbelief, and Afton now held a hand from each of her children. The very last thing she ever would have imagined herself doing was deceiving them. But, for this, she had to. Because they were better off not knowing the truth.

Her children left the house together, just as both of her sisters arrived. Skye led Laney into the living room. They sat close, bookending Afton on one sofa. "Any news from Sam, or the police?" Skye asked first.

Afton shook her head. "They found his car at some shady motel, but other than that, no leads."

"God, this is so bizarre," Laney spoke up.

"Aft, have you said anything to the police about Jess? I mean, come on, considering that they were involved, and he was sort of blackmailing her since Mark died. She could be involved in Sam's disappearance." Afton wished now she had never sent that detailed text to both of them. But there was no way to change that. She would only keep moving forward, and protect Jess in the process.

"You to have to swear to me that you will tell no one about Jess and Sam. Promise me!" Afton insisted.

"Okay," Skye obliged.

"Don't look at me like that," Laney said to Afton as she glared at her. "No one knows anything at school."

"We promise to keep Jess out of this, for whatever reason," Skye stated, "but you have to tell us what's going on. If the police knew what went down with you and Jess and Sam these last few weeks, they would look no further than right here for the answers. What happened Aft?"

Afton paused. "Someday I will share it with both of you. But, for now, I don't want you involved. If the police seek either of you, asking questions, you will only have so much to offer. I want to keep it that way. For now, but not forever. Just let this settle."

"You're protecting us," Laney said.

Afton smiled. "I guess the three of us have really stepped up this sisterhood thing." She liked that very much.

"We are here for you," Skye squeezed her knee.

A few hours after Afton left Jess' house on that fateful day, she called Knox and asked him to meet her on the walking trail at Mears Park. It was early evening when he found her sitting on their special bench.

She was reserved, but he could immediately tell that something was wrong. She kept her voice low when he sat down beside her and rubbed her leg with his open palm.

"Something's happened," she began. "I'm going to report Sam as missing."

"Do you know where he is though?" It was as if Knox could read her mind. That both comforted and scared her at this point.

"He tried to kill me." Afton pointed to the visible red markings at the base of her neck that she hoped would fade within the next twenty-four hours. Before she contacted the police. "Jess was there. She saved my life, Knox."

"And now the two of you share a secret?"

"I'll understand if this is going to be a deal breaker for us," Afton told him, as she held her breath. Any sane person would pick up and freaking run at this point.

"I see it as you could marry me, and as your husband I would be exempt from ever testifying against you in a court of law." He smiled. And she felt like crying. *This man.*

"Hold that thought, okay?" she asked him.

"Absolutely," he put his arm around her, and she let herself fall into him. He was a safe harbor for her. And then she heard him say, "No pressure. You can tell me when you're ready."

"I could be watched for awhile. I don't want to put you in the middle if my privacy is invaded by the authorities."

"I'll take that risk if you are willing to," he stated, without a doubt in his mind. Separating himself from her was not an option. Especially not now — when she obviously needed him the most.

They left the park together that day.

Since Afton and Jess parted that day, they had not seen each other. To anyone else, they were longtime friends. And Jess was that friend, right now, who stopped by to check on Afton amid the news that her husband was missing.

When Afton welcomed her inside, Jess was far from the mind over matter state that Afton had mastered the past couple of days. Or perhaps, Afton had always been good at covering up her true feelings. Learning something new and different about herself had been the norm lately.

"How are you?" Afton asked her, as they stood in her kitchen, and she offered her a seat at the island. "Can I get you some water or something?"

"Something stronger, please," Jess replied.

"I know how this feels," Afton spoke to her, "but you have to hold it together. Alcohol will make the truth spill out a little too freely. Be careful, Jess. Keep your walls up. I'm just saying..."

"I killed a man," her voice was raspy as she spoke. That truth, she believed, most certainly justified her to be worse off than Afton in this predicament.

"And then we united from that moment forward. Focus on that. You are not alone, and we are not going backward. One step at a time. We've got this."

Jess inhaled a slow, deep breath as Afton gave her a glass of iced water. "Have the police been here a lot?"

"A few times, yes, but that's expected. This was his home, and I am the one who reported Sam as missing. I'm retelling the same story each time to make it look like Sam got himself into some trouble with the wrong whore, or skipped town with one."

Jess winced at the thought. She strongly believed that Sam had only cheated with her. Leaving his car at the motel had been a smart move.

"Jess, be confident as the police have no reason to connect you to Sam. You don't have neighbors in close proximity who could have ever seen the two of you together. There's absolutely no trace for we what did that day."

"I just want enough time to pass, so I can put the estate on the market." Afton also planned to move out of the home she shared with Sam. *One day she would.* "Afton... do you ever think about if things were different, if we had just chosen to call the police and claimed self defense?"

"Sure, I do," she answered, truthfully, "but then I think how that would have allowed Sam to win. He could have ruined us both, even in death. Turns out he was a bully who lost. Jess, we got him. Everything is going to be okay. Just ride this out with me."

Jess reached for Afton's hand across the countertop on the island. She held it back with intensity. *Some things were proven to be stronger than the truth.*

Chapter 23

Two weeks later, Afton had heard from Detective Weh only twice. The investigation remained active, but there weren't any new leads. If Sam had willingly left town, there was no trace through his existing credit cards or cell phone. Afton breathed another secret sigh of relief.

She joined her sisters for dinner, with plans to stay the night with Knox later. She still only went to his house on Holly Avenue. Having him in the house she shared with Sam wasn't something Afton was ready for, and she probably never would be. That house was going to eventually be a part of her past.

"You seem well," Laney acknowledged as they sipped glasses of Moscato prior to dinner.

"As well as can be expected," Skye stated, "considering how much your life has continued to change in recent months."

Afton nodded in reference to both of their comments. "I am doing fine. Change is challenging sometimes, but it's easier to take when I know my life is going in a better, healthier direction."

"You have a good support system now," Laney stated, and Skye chimed in. "We assume you're still seeing him — even though you are incredibly private about it."

Afton laughed. "Still am indeed." Both of her sisters wondered if the man in Afton's life knew what they didn't yet, but neither asked. That subject was sealed on Afton's terms.

"Will we ever get to meet him?" Skye asked first, but Laney had already thought it.

"I hope so. You'll love him, I know."

"Are we using the L-word?" Skye thought she was onto something as Laney giggled behind the rim of her wine glass.

"He has," Afton confessed. It had happened once, almost as if it was by the pure accident of being caught up in overwhelming physical and sexual emotion. They had just been intimate, and Knox held nothing back when he verbally expressed that he loved her as he held her afterward. And Afton would always remember what she said in response. "You have to know I feel that emotion from you each time you touch me, or simply look at me. I hope that I'm able to give that back to you in the very same way. And I wish for that to be enough for now," she told him, as she just was not ready to say the words. Afton then reassured him of her unspoken words with her body. And Knox hadn't asked for anything more.

"You're not ready, or you don't quite feel the same yet?" Laney pried.

"Neither," Afton's response was honest. "I'm just taking this newness in my life one moment at a time. I think I deserve to do that for myself."

"Absolutely, you do," Skye spoke and they all were in agreement. Finally, Afton was living her life for herself.

Six weeks had passed. The newness of Afton's life without Sam was beginning to settle in her mind. Like the foundation of a structure that shifted and steadied over time, this change for her was a gradual sink. She still did some things the very same way. She brewed enough coffee for two every morning, and later threw out the rest. She bought white bread at the grocery store, even though she never ate it. His clothes in the walk-in closet remained hanging across from hers. There were things she didn't realize she would miss, and she assumed she would feel the very same if they had gotten divorced. Nothing had brought her to her knees. It was just little things that happened and entered her mind to remind her of the man she shared her life with for more than two decades.

Their daughter Amy was in a new relationship that was suddenly progressing fast, as they had already moved in together. Afton started to think how within reach it now was for her to get married and have babies, or maybe even the other way around. Sam would never have the chance to be a grandfather now. Afton once imagined him to be good in that role. He had always been a doting father when their kids were little. It's when they became teenagers that he withdrew from their real-life problems. It was as if he no longer knew how to make time for the guidance and the advice. He hadn't invested in them anymore, because they weren't as easily entertained or appeased as when they were children. They stopped growing then as a family, Afton recognized, which had forced her to try harder to contain what was left of their unity. She had done everything she could to give her children the balance of structure and stability with love.

Latch, especially, had grown apart from all of them. When he chose not to go to college, Afton thought Sam would follow through with his threat to disown him. He all but did, really. Emotionally, there was no longer any effort put into their father-son relationship. *No son of mine is going waste his life away as an auto body mechanic.* Those words had never been taken back. And couldn't be now.

Afton was walking on uneven, cobblestone pavers downtown Saint Paul. There was another thriving business district separate from where her studio was located. On her path now, she was approaching the auto body shop that Latch owned and operated. He had worked there since he was a teenager. And when the owner, who hired him as practically a kid, eventually decided to retire, Latch bought the business from him. She saw the bank at the intersection ahead, where Latch had gotten his first major loan to make that happen. She then focused on the business her son owned. *Latch Auto Body.* He always loved his first name, even as a little boy, and Afton beamed every time he told her that. Her father's name was Latch. Latch Gallant was a good, honest, trustworthy man. Latch not only resembled him with his lean body, prominent cheek bones, and boyish blond hair — but he was of the same good, honest character too. Her son was very much unlike Sam Drury. And that actually saddened Afton now.

As she came closer to the auto body shop, Afton saw a car backing out of the garage. It was slow to roll, and she spotted her son walking alongside of the driver's open window. That was old-fashioned service that this world didn't see too much of anymore, Afton believed. She wasn't close enough to hear their swapped words, but she imagined Latch was appreciative, and would shake the man's hand and send him on his way. Afton watched Latch bend forward, closer to the window. He rested his forearms there, close to the young male driver, Afton could see them clearer now. And then what she witnessed next caught her breath. They shared a same-sex kiss. On the mouth. Her son kissed, and was kissed by, another man. It was a full-on, open-mouth kiss.

Afton stopped. She froze to the point of not being able to move. *Her boy had always been shy and reserved around girls. He hadn't dated much, if at all, because he wasn't attracted to women. Latch was gay.* Afton started to cry. It's not that she didn't —and wouldn't— support her son no matter what. She was just taken aback. *Did she really know her children? Had she somehow failed to earn their trust?*

She began to walk hard and fast. The bottoms of her feet hurt through the thin soles of her flip-flops. She was adjacent to the funeral home now. So much of that place was still Mark Robertson. The exterior of that three-story building was exquisite and flawless — from the pale red brick, the white shutters bordering every window, to the flower garden landscape around the entire premises. Afton was crying for her son right now. And for a dear friend, a good man gone too soon. Then she thought of Sam. And the significance of the end of his existence at that very funeral home.

It was Jess' impulse plan. Mark's full-size, black, Cadillac Escalade had still been parked in their garage. It's what he drove as his work vehicle. The back of it was without seats. There were folded body bags stored in there for when he had to *pick up a customer*, he used to say.

Somehow, but not without a serious struggle, both Jess and Afton managed to put Sam's body into one of those bags. Afton could still hear the zipper, sticking at times, as they sealed him in there. Jess then drove them to the funeral home downtown.

They made their way around to the back of the building. Afton sat quiet and still in the passenger seat as Jess effortlessly backed the vehicle down a slanted ramp that led up against a pair of double doors. No one was there. Mark's cousin was dividing his time between the funeral home he operated in Minneapolis, and picking up the added business in Saint Paul. That was their temporary solution to fill Mark's place as the owner and director. Jess had backed down that ramp a time or two before. She also had possession of Mark's keys to open those double doors.

They conveniently moved the body bag directly from the vehicle to a gurney-like table on wheels that was made of all stainless steel. In the basement of the funeral home was the morgue. Afton watched Jess preheat the crematory as if it was her own wall oven in her home kitchen. Only the temperature of it was set dangerously high at 1400 degrees Fahrenheit. The intense heat, Jess explained in detail, would reduce the body to its basic elements and dried bone fragments. If Afton would have dwelled on that, right then and there, she would have gotten sick to her stomach. Jess had somehow been able to focus solely on what she was doing. Her state of panic and uncertainty appeared to have dissipated.

They didn't strip Sam's body, nor did they remove his watch or wedding ring, wallet or cell phone. All of it, all of the evidence would burn in the flames of the cremation chamber along with the body of a man that would now never be found.

Almost three hours later, the pile of remains on a single tray was dust, nothing but white particles of dust, along with foreign elements of clothing and metal. Some things had not completely burned or broken down, and Afton helped Jess dump and scrape everything from the tray into a simple trash bag. If either of them would have had time to stop and think about what they were actually doing, it would have brought them to sobs. That man, at one point or another in both of their lives, was someone special to them. Despite how their story ended.

That trash bag with Sam's cremated remains had later gone home with Afton. She could still see herself, less than twelve hours later, placing that bag curbside at her home. When the trashman gathered it, along with a few other bags of garbage to avoid any sole attention going to that one bag, Afton had watched from her front picture window. The giant arm of the truck had churned, rotated, and smashed that one single bag into a mix of nasty trash that would eventually be buried at a landfill. Sam Drury's remains would forever be lost.

There were clusters of unsettling thoughts racing in every direction in her mind right now. Her son's secret would forever change their family. She could accept him. But it broke her heart knowing he hadn't trusted his own mother enough to reveal his true self. But Afton had no right to blame Latch, or shame him. She, too, had lied to her own children. Their father was dead, and she played a role in making sure he disappeared without a trace. She sobbed as she practically ran across the cobblestones under her feet. And then she suddenly lost her footing and went down. She heard something on her body make a loud popping sound, and then she felt an intense pain shoot through her knee. No one was near her, so she forced herself up alone and limped to a bench at least ten feet away in the grass. Her knee had already stiffened too much to bend without a struggle.

She sat down, as tears were streaming off her face. Cars passed by. No one saw, or cared if they did witness her distress. She reached for her cellphone in the pocket of her white capri denim that were now ripped at the knee from her fall. She couldn't call her son. He was just a block and a half away, but she wasn't ready to face him yet. She wasn't given the chance to be there for him when he needed her. She imagined his agony and confusion when he first realized he was different. But he had never reached out to her.

Afton dialed Skye's number. She answered after the first ring.

"Hey big sis…what kind of trouble are in in now?" It was a joke. Skye meant nothing by it, but her words had brought more tears to Afton's eyes.

"I'm hurt," her voice cracked when she choked out those words.

"My God, what's wrong? Where are you?"

"I think I did something awful to my knee. I was walking downtown, near Latch's shop, when I fell on the sidewalk."

"Are you still there?"

"I'm on a bench across the street from Robertson Funeral Home." Skye's first thought was that place had to be difficult for Afton to even look at now. Little did she know the absolute truth to that.

"I'm leaving now. Stay put! I will get you to the ER to be checked out."

"Wait. Skye, not the ER. Take me to Regional Minneapolis. Knox will help me."

Skye stopped racing through her house at that moment. She had her handbag on her shoulder and was about to grab her car keys off the kitchen counter.

Regional Minneapolis.

Knox.

The doctor in the hospital hallway who she was instantly attracted to, had flirted relentlessly with, and later spent hours at a bar with... all before taking him home. He, somehow, was connected to Afton?

"Who's Knox?" Skye was careful to ask.

"I thought I told you he was an orthopedic surgeon. I guess I just never shared his name," Afton slightly giggled, but this wasn't funny. Her knee hurt like hell right now.

Skye also didn't find any of this the least bit comical. *Knox was the man Afton was involved with for months. They were having mind-blowing sex.* Skye left her house, forcing herself to focus on rescuing Afton and getting her some help. She was going to try much harder to convince her sister to go to the ER instead.

Chapter 24

Skye was able to persuade Afton to go to the emergency room first, to possibly have an X-ray and simply know what she was dealing with before she reached out to her orthopedic surgeon boyfriend. It made sense to Afton, but she had insisted on going to the ER at Regency Minneapolis. There, she sent Knox a text while they were seated in the waiting room.

I'm a klutz. I hurt my knee, and I would like for you to take a look at it. I'm under your same roof, in the ER.

Skye watched Afton beside her, occupied on her phone. "Did you let him know that you're here?" Skye couldn't even say his name. Her sister would shun her forever if she ever found out what happened. She had to get to him, without Afton around, and swear him to secrecy.

"I did. You said you wanted to meet him, so now's your chance." Afton's right leg was stretched out in front of her chair. She had to keep from bending it, or the pain was worse.

"How bad does it hurt?"

"I think you know, otherwise I wouldn't be in the ER. Thank you for helping me. I didn't know who else to call."

"I'll take that as a compliment," Skye grinned, "but I am curious why you didn't just hobble over to Latch's shop."

Afton thought again about what she saw. She closed her eyes for a moment, and tried to erase the shock of it that was still there in her mind. *She was his mother.* Nothing felt lower than being the last one to know.

"What is it? You have that look on your face that you get when you're bothered by something. Is there news about Sam?"

"No," Afton shook her head, and thought, *thank goodness, no.* "And, I didn't want to bother Latch, as he's working."

"You can't even say your son's name right now without looking pained."

"It's my knee," Afton tried to detour from the subject of Latch.

"You're forgetting that I know you pretty well. Tell me what's going on. Laney and I both have been more than patient with you and the things you choose to keep to yourself." She was referring to Sam's sudden disappearance.

And Afton knew Skye had made a valid point.

"Okay, I saw Latch. He was with a young man, a customer, I assumed. He bent forward into this man's car window and they shared a pretty steamy kiss."

"Latch?" Skye's eyes widened. They both kept their voices down in that waiting room, even though it was not overly crowded at midday.

"I had no idea." Afton admitted, and her eyes were teary.

Skye instantly reaching for her hand. "So are you okay with that, I mean, that he's apparently gay…"

"I am," Afton nodded her head, "but I'm hurt that he didn't think he could confide in me."

"Oh Aft, I'm so sorry…" Skye was going to wrap her arm around her big sister's shoulder, but that gesture of comfort was interrupted when Afton's name was called by the nurse. "Do you want me to wait here?" Skye wished they could separate for awhile to lessen the risk of seeing Knox now that he knew Afton was there.

"You can come along, if you want," Afton told her, and Skye stood up to walk with her.

In the exam room, Skye found a chair along the wall as Afton had her knee checked out by a physician's assistant. She bent it as he asked, and as much as she could tolerate, as she answered all of the pertinent questions. The PA suspected that she only sprained her knee, and that nothing appeared to be torn or broken. He ordered an X-ray to be certain, and told her to wait there.

"Lucky girl. Looks like you won't be needing your boyfriend's special skills." Skye wished they would get out of there before he made his way from the third floor, down to the ER. Yes, she remembered that his office was located on the third floor. Better yet, she hoped he was busy with a surgery, and she had no idea where the OR was located.

Afton smiled. "Knox *is* really special to me. He's changed me and my life in so many ways." Skye watched her sister speak. *She was in love.*

"He's a lucky man, too. You've held back for too long. It's time to live, Aft."

"I'm working on that." Nothing could be rushed right now, but Afton would sell the house eventually. She also wanted to reach out to her son, and have a heartfelt talk with him. And with her daughter, too, for that matter. They needed to unite as a family again. Just as she and her sisters had reconnected and grown closer.

Two knocks sounded on the glass sliding door which was covered by a solid green curtain that Afton thought resembled the standard hue of hospital scrubs. They were both expecting a nurse to take Afton for her X-ray. But when the door slid open on its floor track, Afton and Skye both were looking at Knox Manning in a white lab coat. He first made eye contact with Afton. "Hey... what happened to you?" His smile was one of compassion and concern as he took two strides to get to her, as he casually glanced over at the chair along the wall to see who was there. He felt his face fall. His heart rate quickened. He quickly looked down at Afton, and then back over at the woman seated against the wall. There was a resemblance. Similar round faces. A bridge of freckles across their noses. Hazel eyes. Knox forced himself to focus on Afton. He bent down to the floor in front of her.

"I went for a walk downtown, I got distracted on the cobblestones, and fell. I'm being told that it's only a sprain."

Knox carefully put his hands on her swollen knee. He turned her leg side to side, and was cautious how far to bend it until she reacted. "I can't bend it back all the way without having to stop," Afton explained.

"It's not loose at all, and that's a good sign. No tears. Just bruised in there pretty good. Ice and elevate, and take ibuprofen too, you hear?"

She smiled at him. "Only if you'll be there with me," she spoke, not caring that Skye was in the room with them, and then she realized she was indeed being rude. "Oh my gosh, my manners are awful. Knox, meet my baby sister, Skye Gallant."

It was her. He instantly had flashed to meeting her in the hospital hallway. Semi-short navy blue business skirt, open-collared white blouse. They met up later at the bar. They talked. They flirted. Sex on her sofa had ended the night, and ceased their contact with each other. A one-night stand. Knox had regretted it. But, God, he had no idea that it would ever come back to haunt him like this. *He slept with Afton's sister.*

Knox swallowed hard, the lump rising in his throat. "Hello Skye. Very nice to meet you." He never made any attempt to walk over to her, to politely reach for her hand. And Skye surely didn't want him to.

"Yes, good to finally meet you, too," Skye spoke. Afton was oblivious to the panicked glances that shot back and forth between the two of them.

"Is there a restroom close by that I could use?" Skye stood up. She had to get out of there.

Knox understood her need to flee. "Down the hall, second door on your left."

"Be right back," Skye looked at Afton. But she had no intention of rushing to return to that room with him. And her sister. Together. *What had she done...*

"She rescued me today," Afton spoke gratefully of Skye.

"I'm glad," Knox cleared his thoughts, and stood up. "Listen, you really do need to take good care of that knee for the next forty-eight hours or so. Can I talk you into staying with me? I'm good with playing doctor..."

She giggled, before she grew serious. "I want that so much. Thank you. Yes, I'll stay with you." Knox reached for her hand, brought it to his lips and kissed her fingers.

"I have to get back to my rounds. Stay after your X-ray and I will bring you home. Right knee. You shouldn't be driving."

"Skye is driving. Just go back to where you're needed for now. Maybe you can pick me up at home later?"

"I'd like that," he said, smiling.

When he left the room, he sealed the sliding glass door and privacy curtain again. A second later, the nurse who was going to bring Afton to her X-ray, reopened it and peeked her head inside. "Be back in three minutes. I haven't forgotten about you, hon." Afton nodded and smiled.

The curtain wasn't closed all the way now. Afton could see the back of Knox's white lab coat across the hall. He was talking to someone. He shifted his body on his two feet and then Afton could also see Skye.

"Not here," were the first words that Skye spoke to him when they were facing each other in the hallway. The single restroom was occupied, so she had turned around and walked back. "We can't have this conversation here." *Or ever, if she had a choice.*

"Afton can't know," he immediately responded.

"I completely agree. Just forget it happened." Skye was fidgeting with the wide strap of her handbag.

"Right." Knox was staring. He still couldn't believe it. *They were sisters.*

How awkward.

"I have to go," Knox spoke again. And he walked past her without another word from him or her.

Sans audio, Afton watched that exchange. If she had to describe what she saw, it would be the body language of two anxious people. Not necessary strangers either. She creased her brow as she watched them for those brief moments. And then the nurse returned before Afton could decipher what just happened out there. *It was probably nothing. Nothing at all.*

Chapter 25

The X-ray was clear of any obvious damage to her knee. Afton had Skye drive her home so she could begin her regime of rest. Until Knox arrived. It would be his first time there. At her house. The home she shared with Sam. But Sam was gone now. And this step with Knox, as she invited him to see a closer glimpse of her world, would be good for her.

Skye helped Afton get settled on the reclining end of one of the sofas in her living room. She had an ice pack over her knee and she promised to rest. "Okay, you have what you need, right?"

"Yes, please go be a mommy to that baby girl of yours. I've taken up enough of your time."

"I do have to pick her up, but call me if you need me to come back for anything." Skye was anxious to get out of that house before Knox arrived. All Afton had spoken about on the way there was him coming over for the first time.

"Knox will be here soon," Afton smiled.

"Right. Knox." Skye really had to get going.

"What do you think of him? Do you see the age difference?"

"No, not at all. Don't fret over something so trivial. You care about each other — that's what matters." He obviously had fallen hard for Afton. Skye could have picked up on the chemistry between them with her eyes closed.

"Good. I like hearing that. Now, go. And thank you again!" Afton called out after her.

The moment the front door was closed, Afton remembered her cell phone left in the kitchen. She moved the ice pack aside on the sofa cushion and carefully stood up to limp in there to get it. She saw from her picture window that Knox had shown up.

Skye was about to get inside her vehicle, as Knox was walking up the driveway. His car was parked along the curb on the street. Afton watched them again.

"You're turn," Skye said, in reference to caring for Afton. She wanted to keep their interaction light. "She's on the sofa, elevated with ice, as instructed." Her car door was open. She wanted to leave.

"Should we talk about this... about what happened between us? Skye, I am in love with your sister. If she knew that we—"

Skye raised her hand in the air between them. "No. We don't need to rehash anything. It was one night. Afton would never understand. Trust me. We have to erase it. Or we will both lose her."

Knox nodded. They were on the same page. "Thank you. I just didn't want you to think of me as someone who would ever intentionally deceive Afton. I regretted what we did ever since it happened. It didn't mean anything." *Great. That made her feel like the whore she acted like sometimes.* The fact was, Skye hadn't been with another man since. She felt remorseful for the way she used Knox that night. He was different than other men who only wanted to get her into bed. They genuinely connected, while they shared nice and easy conversation. Then she rode his lap on her sofa, before he bent her over it. She recalled practically pushing him out the door afterward. The expression on his face had stayed with her.

"Think nothing of it. Go inside. My sister is waiting for you."

Knox backed away, as Skye hurried to sit behind the wheel and she watched him sprint up the driveway to be with Afton.

Afton never made it into the kitchen. She was back on the sofa when Knox knocked twice before he opened the door and slowly stepped inside. When he saw her, he said, "Okay if I let myself in?"

"I would get up, but—" she gestured to her injured knee underneath the ice pack again.

"Stay put," he pointed back at her, as he walked over to sit down beside her. Knox looked around the living room a little, and she noticed.

"Is it weird for you to be here?" she asked him.

"Not really. Probably weirder for you to have me here, don't you think?"

She nodded. There was no risk of Sam ever walking through that door again. She briefly let her mind revert to her breakdown on the sidewalk near the Robertson Funeral Home. Something like that could haunt a person forever. If she allowed it. "It is, but he isn't coming back. I've accepted that, and I'm moving on with my life."

Knox still wanted to know what in the hell happened to that man. He didn't have to guess that it was bad. Really bad. It should have bothered him to know that Afton was keeping a secret from him, one that she likely shared with Jess Robertson. But it didn't consume him. Especially not now, as he and Skye were sharing silence about getting together in the full sense. Strangely, he wished to never know Afton's secret. Because that could somehow justify him also hiding something from her. *God he was an idiot for letting that ever happen. No matter whose sister she was. It was reckless and wrong.*

"Hold onto to all of that," Knox touched her hand. "Move on with your life. Start over with me."

She winked at him and he leaned in for a slow, tender kiss. And then she pulled away. "Take me back to your place for more of that," she suggested, and he understood.

"We should pack a few things for you then," he stood up, ready to go up the stairs or wherever she directed him.

"Already taken care of, courtesy of Skye. My bag is in the kitchen."

"She's a good sister." At first, those were just words strewn together to make conversation. But Knox caught himself after he spoke. His face felt flushed, but he didn't think Afton had noticed.

"We're ten years apart, so growing up it was difficult to be super close. She was always a baby to me." Knox was closer in age to Skye than he was to Afton. She was younger, thinner, sexier. She could still bear another child, maybe. That thought was what bothered her when she saw the two of them together. Twice. What if Knox had a better offer? She and Knox had never been around anyone else when they were together. It was always just the two of them. She had not seen him interact with other women. He was attentive to Skye. And, yes, that bothered Afton more than she wanted to admit.

"I see the kin resemblance with you two," Knox safely commented.

"She's beautiful," Afton stated.

"So are you."

"She can have any man she wants, really."

Knox immediately felt uncomfortable. Obviously he had known there was truth to that. "Is she attached?" he asked, standing near the sofa where Afton still had her leg propped up.

"Her relationships are fleeting. She doesn't commit." Afton tried not to talk negatively about Skye. "She has a baby, but the father is not in the picture. She enjoys sort of a free lifestyle, with the exception of being a mother — which was entirely her choice." The awkward part about this conversation for Knox, other than the obvious, was that he already knew most of what Afton was telling him about Skye.

"Knox, can I ask you something?" he put his hands in the side pockets of his dress pants and rocked on his heels. This was a nervous reaction of his. "If we have a future together, will you regret not finding a woman who could still give you a child?"

He had thought of it, he wasn't going to lie. But there was an undeniable force of nature between him and Afton. He wanted her. And she would have to be enough. "I love you, Afton."

He had only said that to her one other time. She swallowed hard the lump that wanted to take over her throat. "But sometimes love isn't enough. We both know that, don't we?"

He walked over to her, and knelt down on the tweed area rug in front of her. He placed his palms on each side of her face, forcing her to look him in the eye. "It's enough with us. Believe that. And know that I never want any other woman taking up space in my heart. Only you." Knox had to say those words aloud, especially now. He wanted to redeem himself in his own mind. *He loved her. Now and always.*

Afton looked away. Her focus was on the mantle high on the wall across the room. There were photographs, many of them, of her family. Her kids when they were small. Significant events like birthdays, formal dances, high school graduation, and dental school. She still left the photos of Sam up there, too. He was a part of their story. "My son's name is Latch. He owns an auto body shop, downtown. My daughter, Amy, is a dental hygienist."

Knox remained on his knees on the area rug at her feet. "I know all of that. You've shared it with me."

"Yes, but I haven't shared them with you. There is so much of me, and I'm certain there also is so much of you, that we aren't aware of or just do not share."

"That's part of getting to know each other. We fell into this pretty fast, and it's all been just between us, as it should be. But, now, we are beginning to fill in the rest of those blanks. That's just how relationships work sometimes, I guess. There's no blueprint for how it has to be done, Afton."

"And that's also why sometimes people go their separate ways. You get to know someone, the realness about who they are, and you change your mind. It's like buying something at the store, and later deciding to return it. It didn't fit that way the first time I had it on my body. It doesn't look right on me after all."

"I happen to believe we fit together in the most perfect way, and that couldn't feel truer to me." Afton was about to interrupt to tell him that a relationship cannot survive on sex alone. That eventually fades, or so she had assumed. She had never enjoyed being physical with any man like this ever before. Instead of interrupting him, though, she listened. "I know you feel the same way. This is just normal panic setting in. We are on an unknown path together, and for someone like you who has followed a well-beaten one her whole life, this is serious change. I understand. There is no rush for us to learn everything there is to know about each other — unless you want to play a quick game of truth or dare."

That was the wrong thing to say. Knox instantly caught himself.

"Truth," she said to him, and there was a sudden seriousness in her voice and in her eyes.

Knox played along.

"Sam is dead, isn't he?"

She paused.

Knox wasn't asking her what happened, what she and Jess had done to cause a man to go missing for days and weeks on end to date.

"Yes," she answered, in barely a whisper.

Knox inhaled a long, deep breath. It's not like he hadn't suspected as much. And then it was Afton's turn. *Truth or Dare?*

She looked him in the eyes, and he told her, "Truth..."

She heard herself ask him what had been on the forefront of her mind since the moment she saw the two of them through that parted curtain in the hospital ER. And again, outside of her window, on her driveway. It was impossible to ignore the intensity between them that they were unable to mask.

"Have you and my sister met before today?

Chapter 26

Knox moved from his knees to his rear on the area rug. He needed to steady himself. He believed that keeping something from someone, something that could hurt them, was very different than lying outright. But, if he answered Afton now, and told her they had never met before, that would be a lie.

He couldn't lie to her — just as Afton had not lied when she told him that Sam was dead. Knox wanted to justify that being involved in someone's demise and then somehow covering it up was far worse than sleeping with his lover's sister. But he knew Afton wouldn't see it that way at all.

His silence scared her. She wanted to say, *You're not answering me.* Or, *how do you know Skye?* But she was afraid of what she might continue to ask him if she were on a roll with her questions. *Had he slept with her?* Skye didn't have male friends or acquaintances.

This wasn't going to be fair to Skye. They had just wholeheartedly agreed to take that secret to their graves. And now, Knox had to break that pact — and risk both of their relationships with Afton.

"I met Skye at Regency Minneapolis. She was on her way to a meeting with the PR director. The hospital was looking to revamp their website." Already, Afton realized that Knox knew more about Skye that she had told him. "I pointed her in the right direction. We talked."

"You mean she flirted, she came onto you right there in the hospital, didn't she?"

Knox had to tell her the truth. "Later the same day, we bumped into each other in the elevator. She asked me out. And we met up for a drink that evening."

"Did you sleep with her?" Afton wanted to be spared the details of what they talked about or where they were before it happened. Because, yes, she already knew it happened. The fact that they hid their initial meeting with each other from her, told her all she needed to know.

"I followed her back to her place." The color drained from Knox's face. He was so ashamed. Even before now, he had regretted that night. "It was empty sex. It was quick and meaningless. I left immediately. She wanted me out right then. I felt used, even though I was a willing participant. It's never happened again. Not with anyone. And it never will. I haven't seen your sister again until today."

Afton felt numb. She wanted him out. Out of her house, and out of her life. But, first, she had one more thing that she needed to hear from him.

"When did this happen?" If he told her that he had sex with her sister before he met her, it still wouldn't matter. But she feared that was not the story.

"You and I had been together one time. It's irrelevant for me to say that I didn't know if we had a chance, if you would want to see me again. You were married. It was complicated."

"So while you were waiting for me to make up my mind… after you told me you would wait for me…you were having a little fun. Empty sex, as you said?"

"It wasn't like that. Afton, the moment it happened, I could only think of you and how being with you was what I wanted in my life. I want to make love and feel close to the woman I love afterward."

Love. She was relieved she had never said it. Never spoke what she did feel in her heart and soul. She loved him. But, damn it, she would never tell him now.

"Please understand. I didn't know she was your sister. I am not a man who sleeps around. It was wrong."

"Trust is sort of foreign to me. My marriage had very little of it. I don't openly confide in too many people. It's just who I am. But you were different, at least I thought you were. You were a breath of fresh air. I found myself drawn to those exclusive feelings. I fell for the way it felt to have an open conversation with someone, where emotions surfaced and were shared. And I wanted more. I was finally able to freely give myself, body and soul, to someone for the first time. And it was liberating."

Knox felt tears spill over from his eyes. He knew that he destroyed the foundation they had just built together. And it was a solid one. Until he handed her the tools to destroy it. The fault was his own.

"Trust can be rebuilt," he spoke, because he had to take a chance. It was the last one within his grasp.

"I want you to go."

The vast difference between Knox and Sam brought hot tears to her eyes once he was gone. Knox hadn't reacted with denial, with rage, or with a ridiculous claim of ownership. He had just given up and walked away. At this point, Afton didn't know which hurt worse.

Chapter 27

The very next day, Afton's knee had already felt more bendy and less painful. She cut short any need to rest and take care of the bruising. She didn't care.

More than just her knee was bruised anyway. The ache in her heart was the worst. But she pressed on.

First, she asked her son if she could bring coffee to his shop, before business hours. They sat in a small, cluttered office which was surrounded by glass walls in the far corner of the massive garage with nice cars, junkier cars, and merely car parts. The smell in there, Afton processed, was a combination of fresh paint and oil. Her son was quiet, at first, which was the typical boy she raised and absolutely adored. Afton began by telling him that she believed she had failed as his mother. She too was often afraid of open communication and genuine emotion. Though she loved both him and his sister and mothered them with everything she could possibly give, it had not been enough. They were now detached from her as young adults. Latch had tried to argue her point, her feelings that had come out of nowhere at him. But she asked him to listen, long and hard. Afton told him what she saw, just a day ago, and he closed down. He couldn't even look at her. She only talked more. She held nothing back. Latch heard from his mother that she was stunned at first, and then the hurt came. A son should be able to tell his mother what's going on in his mind and heart. And if he had confided in her, she would have supported him and aided him in every way possible. That still remained a fact. She would always be in her son's corner. Latch had fallen to his knees in front of the chair his mother sat on. And she held him as he sobbed with his head buried in her lap. There was no shame or disappointment. Just a new understanding of her grown son. And perhaps, this could be a new beginning for them, if they both worked very hard at it.

And then Afton reached out to her daughter. Amy was harder to influence. She always had been. She grew up as a daddy's girl, and always preferred Sam to doctor her skinned knees and wipe away her tears. Afton believed she grieved for her father, and the bond they once shared, long before he was truly gone. Afton talked, and kept talking, until Amy gave in. She refused to cry. She was so much like her mother. But she did admit to Afton that she struggled with commitment. She claimed to have mirrored her aunt Skye more than she wanted to. Men were fleeting. This boyfriend in her life now, however, had taught her to believe in fidelity and trust. That was why she had taken the leap with him, and they were now living together. Afton stood in that apartment with her daughter, and began to see a different side to the young woman she had raised. She was fearless and strong, and also vulnerable and lost. She would find her way though, and Afton wanted to be as much a part of that journey with her as she would allow.

Last, Afton chose to contact Laney. But not in person. She only called her. Laney was completely caught off guard and listened raptly as she explained what had happened with Knox, and how Skye was involved in the demise of their relationship that was in so many ways just beginning. Afton believed that Knox had not told Skye, because she would have come running and begging and pleading with her. For her understanding. For her forgiveness. Laney would tell her now though. Probably the moment they ended their phone call. Afton could count on that. Not that it mattered anymore. Afton was done trying to figure out who was with her, against her, or walking down the middle because they just never could pick a side. Deep down, she knew her sisters were on her side. They always had been. Just like she was on theirs. She believed Skye would not purposely hurt her. But the need to see her again, to confront her, was not present. Not yet. And it may never be. The act of forgiving and forgetting was just too damn hard sometimes. Sister, or not.

$$\neq$$

Afton had the window seat, and Jess had the aisle. The flight was going to take them to Long Beach, California. Afton had chosen that coastal city as their destination just moments before she called up Jess. It wasn't on a whim, she had thought about getting away, and she had contemplated asking Jess to join her. This trip, the uninterrupted time together, would either bond them further or break them for good. Afton had no idea which, but she was willing to give whatever was left between them — one last try. A part of her truly wanted to fight for the friendship they had never really delved into. They had, however, dove deep as partners in crime. *Literally.* Their shared secret had formed a forever connection between them.

Jess was still unsure exactly why Afton had asked her to join her on a getaway that she explained as being nothing but beach time. She wanted to feel the sand between her toes, the sun on her body, and she intended to swim in the ocean. Jess was drawn to the idea, as she needed to remain focused on finding clarity in her life. There was no turning back, no dwelling or over-analyzing the secret they shared until she reached the point of crazy. And she had already come close a time or two. Even still, Jess remained skeptical of why Afton wanted her along.

After takeoff, Afton glanced from the window to Jess beside her. She had a laptop resting on her legs, and she was intently focused on the screen. Afton zeroed in to read. The word *mortuary* caught her eye. Afton pressed her finger to the laptop's screen. "What are you reading?"

Jess lost her focus. She turned her body partway toward Afton. "I was going to tell you, for sure during all of our time together on this trip. I'm changing careers. I've talked at length with Mark's cousin, the one who I told you is stretched too thin as he's running both funeral homes in the Twin Cities. I've always had an interest in Mark's work." Afton could not help it. Her mind flashed to how effortlessly Jess had worked under pressure in the crematory part of the morgue. "I want to fill Mark's position with the funeral home. I've enrolled in mortuary school. It should take me about two years to earn my degree in mortuary science, and I'm going to complete my apprenticeship during that time with Mark's cousin. I'll work between the two funeral homes with him."

Afton was beyond impressed. "Good for you. I cannot tell you how surprised I am by this." They really had not known each other at all. They were only friends on the surface all those years. "I was worried," Afton kept her voice low. "I could see you sinking after what happened." Afton reached for her leg and patted it. "I'm proud of you for having such strength and for setting goals!"

Jess beamed. "Someone led by example and paved that path for me. It's never too late to begin again."

Afton didn't accept praise very easily, but Jess' words truly had touched her. Afton wondered exactly how much Jess had heard about her attempt to start anew with her own life. Because that path had forked. Seizing a life with Knox Manning was no longer a chance she would chase.

Jess wore a peach bikini on the beach, with a large wide-brimmed straw hat to shade her face from the hot rays. She looked flawless and fit. Afton could have rolled her eyes, as she was wearing a more modest black tankini. Her full breasts and curvy rear looked good, she had to admit, but her middle and her lovies could have used a quick liposuction in places. She wore large, dark sunglass to shield her eyes from the bright sun. Her shoulder-length hair was pulled back. They sat in low, lounge chairs, directly in the sand on the beach. This was day three of their getaway. Afton's skin already had a nice glow. The bridge of freckles across her nose was more prominent, and she had gone without makeup for days. Jess had a perfect tan, but the crow's feet around her eyes had increased a little. She was a squinter in the sun at times, under that hat, as she had only periodically worn sunglasses.

They spent an equal amount of time together the past few days as they had alone. Jess always carted her laptop with her and was studying often. Afton simply relaxed. She called her children daily, and Laney once. Otherwise she had her phone powered off and back on the nightstand beside her bed at the beach house. It was easier to ignore Skye's messages that way. There were several voicemail and texts from her alone. And, while she told herself she didn't care and wasn't even going to look, there was not a single effort from Knox. *That was just as well.* She respected him for not wasting his time, or hers.

Afton saw Jess close the lid on her laptop. She reached between their lounge chairs and into a cooler they shared. She handed her one of their premixed pink lemonade and strawberry vodka drinks which they had poured into their refillable clear cups with long, colored, plastic straws.

"Thank you," Afton took a generous sip and laid her head back against the chair. She closed her eyes and felt the sun on her face.

"We've been enjoying this for days," Jess stated, "we have shared relaxation, small talk, good food and alcohol... and some laughs. This is nice, Afton. I still have to ask you though, why me? Why did you want me, of all people, to be here with you?"

Afton opened her eyes and sat up a little straighter on her lounge chair. Now was as good a time as ever. "I wanted you out of my life the moment I saw you and Sam together. It oddly hurt me more knowing that you betrayed me. I told myself that I didn't need you. Were we really all that close of friends? We weren't. And I had no issue with shutting you out of my life." Afton paused. She wanted to tell her this. "In the middle of the chaos, I had met a man, a little younger than me. I was drawn to him. His intelligence. His compassion. He was a communicator, a touchy-feely kind of man. And sexy as hell. He managed to reach me, or I just gave in, one or the other. I didn't care which. I just wanted to keep feeling the changes he brought out of me. The light he helped me see within myself. In my soul, for chrissakes." The expression on Jess' face could not be hidden. She was utterly shocked. "I admitted I was having an affair, and I told Sam I wanted a divorce. I didn't give a crap if he knew, because he cheated on me too. He refused. His dangerous true colors surfaced quickly and you and I both felt the wrath of it. Jess... you saved my life."

"You saved both of our lives afterward. I think we both know the serious charges we would have faced," Jess stated what she believed was a matter of fact.

"Your quick action was foolproof. The means that we had available was unbelievable." Although it still haunted her at times. "Sometimes I think about it, and just can't believe it. We are bonded because of that. We didn't have to be friends anymore though. I wondered if seeing each other would repeatedly bring it all back. It hasn't," she added.

"Not for me either," Jess admitted. "It's there, but it's not on a constant reel in my mind just because you are sitting next to me."

Afton continued telling her story to Jess. "I found out that my youngest sister had a one-night stand with the man I had fallen for." She still refused to use the word *love* out loud. "Neither of them knew who the other was, or at least their shared connection with me. At that time, I had only been in his bed once. I was married. I was uncertain if we were just having sex and leaving it at that. There are regrets on his part, and my sister's apparently. Doesn't matter now. I don't want either of them in my life anymore."

"That's a lot to carry," Jess began, thinking cautiously before she spoke. Sex was a sore subject between the two of them to say the very least. "Relationships take a lot of work, I don't care who you are. I wish I could change many of my choices in my life, but mostly I wish I had not caused people pain. Mark. I don't know if he ever knew or wondered. Not about me with Sam, in particular, but with any man. And you. I'll forever be the bitch who screwed your husband."

Afton suppressed a giggle.

"It's not funny," Jess reacted.

"It's not," Afton agreed, "but given what we went through with that son of a bitch, I think we have a right to giggle. To just tip back our vodka swishing around in those cups, and let it all go. Yes, you fucked him. I guess somebody had to, because I sure as hell wasn't." They both howled with laughter on that beautiful, peaceful beach.

And when they caught their breaths, Jess spoke first.

"It's none of my business, but you're my friend, so I'm just going to put this out there…" It felt wonderful for both of them to know they were friends. In true, genuine fashion now. Afton listened intently. "Life is fleeting, as we both very well know. We lost Mark. Sam is forever missing. We have our children and one day our grandchildren. But, we are hardly old and feeble and ready to give up on ourselves, and our own lives. We are vibrant women with both simple and complex needs. I need a new purpose to wake up and get moving every morning. You get that rise from photography. And you also have been given the chance to have real love in your life. The kind, from what you have already described to me, that makes the temperature change in the room when he walks in." Afton thought about the very first moment Knox came into her studio. She blamed the humidity and had spiked the air conditioner. "Don't turn your back on that. Sure, mistakes were made. But, you and I know best that there's a way to put pain in the past."

Afton reached up in the space between them with her drink in hand and she clanked her cup with the one Jess held.

No more words were spoken between them for a long while. But the message prior was most definitely heard.

Chapter 28

They had been back from the beach for two weeks. The weather was awful in Saint Paul. Hit or miss rain fell and it was constantly cloudy for days on end. Both Afton and Jess had taken turns texting each other at times, complaining about being back to gloom and doom. They missed the sunshine on the beach, and when Afton suggested they make that trip an annual thing between them, Jess beamed and accepted the invite for all the years to come.

She knew the path at Mears Park, the trail in the heart of downtown Saint Paul's Lowertown district, would be muddy. She imagined the stream running diagonally through that park to be overflowing from the constant rain. But there was finally a break from it when the sun boldly peeked out from behind the clouds. That's when Laney had called her and suggested a walk in the park. Afton accepted, without hesitation. She still needed her sisters in her life. She just had not been sure how or where to start over with Skye.

When Afton parked her vehicle, she saw Laney already there and getting out of hers. And she wasn't alone. Skye was with her. Afton willed herself not to react. Not to flee on the impulse of a bruised heart to get back into her car to speed off and out of there.

Both of her sisters moved toward her, in shared silence.

Skye was always the one to speak first. She was noted for it. This time, however, she was silent. After all of her pleas had been sent and ignored without a single reply, she had given up on speaking her piece. It was Laney who forced her to be there today. She was the middle sister and in the middle of their rift now. But she wasn't going to give up on either of them. Pushing them together, like this, was a start.

Afton was standing toe-to-toe with both of them before she finally spoke. "It's a good feeling to see you two." Skye was teary just hearing Afton include her.

"We've missed you too," Laney spoke for all of them. They all had missed nurturing their sisterhood, especially the closeness that had finally taken off among them.

"We should walk," Afton suggested, as they were standing in the middle of the parking lot.

Once they made it to the trail, Skye touched Afton's hand. She halted in her tracks, and it took her a moment to look up at Skye. The tallest sister of the three. "I will always hate myself for hurting you," Skye began, and she choked on those words as the tears freefell onto her cheeks.

"Hate is a strong word," Afton stated.

"Mom used to say that," Laney reminded them, and they had remembered.

"I don't want you to hate yourself," Afton continued, holding her baby sister's hand. "I don't feel that way about you." She did hate the image of her sister and Knox *together* though. "It's going to take some time, but I want us to make it back to that place we reached not too long ago."

"That *call me when you need me* place. Or, when you're simply thinking of me," Laney stated to both of them. "When something happens in your life, good or shitty, and you want someone to share it with. That's who we need to be together."

Both Afton and Skye used their free hands to reach for Laney. They stood in a circle, linked together. "One step at a time. We can start on this trail," Afton suggested. "And we'll get there, I promise."

"We're so happy to hear you say that," Skye spoke, looking at Laney as if the two of them shared a secret. A part of Afton was miffed. *Not again. Not now.* "We have something special for you. And if we take a little walk here, you'll find what's waiting."

Afton creased her brow. "I don't like surprise gifts. Just give it to me now." Her sisters laughed at her childlike complaining.

"Nope. It will be worth the wait," Laney stated.

They walked, three-wide at times, and single-file during others, depending on how the trail's width altered. When they neared the bench, that special bench, Afton stopped. "I can't," she said to both of her sisters. "I don't trust that I'm ready for this."

Knox was waiting for her in the distance. He never moved. He agreed to be there, but this moment was on Afton's terms. Laney forced Afton to look at both her and Skye. "Listen. None of us are ever ready for what life throws at us. Sometimes it's so good it hurts. You know what you had with him. Don't give that up."

"Don't throw your happiness away because of me..." Skye said, and she looked pained as she spoke those words. "He loves you. It's blatantly obvious in the way he looks at you, and with how patient he's been. He's waiting for you, Aft. Just go. Go to him."

Laney and Skye stood back as Afton walked forward on the trail. Toward the man who would have waited forever for her to change her mind.

She reached the bench, and he stood up for her. "Hi," she spoke first, and this felt incredibly awkward. Her sisters were watching. She wasn't prepared to see him and yet there he was. His hair looked a little shorter, but it was still wavy and disheveled and so perfectly him. That boyish look of a beautiful man remained. She had missed so much about him.

"Hi back," he spoke. "It's really good to see you."

"You too," she replied.

"You're tan," he noted. The freckles on her nose were prominent and it made him smile.

"I went to the beach for awhile."

"Good therapy," he nodded.

"That it was. I took Jess with me. She and I were able to find peace and forgiveness."

"That's hard to do sometimes," Knox was referring to what he had done to her.

"Impossible," Afton added, "but it's freeing if and when you finally find it."

Knox hoped with all of this heart that Afton had found a way to forgive him, or at least to somehow understand that he nor Skye were at fault. Their actions had nothing to do with intentionally hurting her. "I am not here to push you, or plead with you. As hard as it's been, I didn't reach out to you. Time heals some things. I was holding out hope for that. Still am. I don't even care if it's false hope. I just need something to hang on to." Afton noticed the sadness in his eyes as he spoke. She had put that there when she walked away from their chance.

"I've missed you," Afton spoke what was in her heart. "Your smile. Your light. The way you make me feel optimistic about myself and my life." Knox stepped closer to her, but he didn't touch her. Not just yet. "This path that leads to this bench, it's special to us," she noted. "I want to get back on a path with you, any path, I just want to try and see where it leads. If we don't just do it, we'll never know if we could end up somewhere that we want to be."

"I'll jump on any path with you. Even if it's a rocky one, in parts. Just take my hand." She did. And it felt liberating to feel his touch again.

She saw the tears in his eyes. She was not a crier, but she could have just bawled knowing they had made their way back to sharing something so special, so good that it hurt sometimes. Laney's words had resonated with her.

Knox held her in his arms and kissed her senseless. She eventually backed away and glanced, partly embarrassed, at her sisters who made nothing of listening to and watching them. They giggled out loud through their tears and their shared happiness. "You two…" Afton raised her voice at them, "thank you for your scheming part in bringing me back to life, and love, with this man."

About the Author

This story began with the idea of a couple who had grown apart. They coexisted in a life together. But the love was gone. And communication had long ceased. As the lives of the characters unfolded, "shared silence" also became about dishonesty and harboring secrets.

Is keeping something from someone —something that could hurt them and alter lives— different from outright lying? Is it justifiable in your own mind and heart to choose wrongdoing in an effort to protect yourself or others? Are some things stronger than the truth? I based many of the characters in this book on all of those things. And interestingly, I hope that you will find yourselves rooting for them regardless of their right or wrong choices. I know I did.

I ended this story without writing an epilogue. I typically give the reader a glimpse into the future of the characters' lives. This was definitely a happy ending, and I chose to leave it be (for now).

Why? Because a storyline like this reflects true life. We don't always get everything we want in its entirety. Knox yearns to be a father, but we know he probably will not get that chance. Some missing persons cases remain unsolved. Did Sam get what he deserved? Were you rooting for Afton and Jess to ultimately get by with what they did? I may have surprised myself with that shocking twist!

There's also another reason why I decided not to write an epilogue for *Shared Silence*. This summer, I will delve into more of this story. *As We Are* will be a closer look at Laney and Brad's life with their twin boys. I want to also revisit Skye and her baby girl, as well as Jess Robertson. And who knows? There could be more story to tell for Afton and Knox. Look for two more books in 2019 that will focus on the lives of the Gallant sisters who are all undoubtedly intricate and unpredictable women. *As We Are* will be released in August 2019, with *For Reasons Unknown* to follow in October/November 2019. This will be my first trilogy!

I continue to be grateful for the inspiration and creativity that never stops. And I am forever appreciative of my readers who are endlessly ready and waiting for more.

As always, thank you for reading!

love,

Lori Bell

Made in the USA
Columbia, SC
24 May 2019